THE
SOUL SNATCHER

THE
SOUL SNATCHER

PHIL TOMLINSON

Matador
9 Priory Business Park
Kibworth Beauchamp
Leicestershire LE8 0RX, UK
Tel: (+44) 116 279 2299
Fax: (+44) 116 279 2277
Email: books@troubador.co.uk
Web: www.troubador.co.uk/matador

ISBN 978 1780882 895

British Library Cataloguing in Publication Data.
A catalogue record for this book is available from the British Library.

Typeset in 11pt Book Antiqua by Troubador Publishing Ltd, Leicester, UK
Printed and bound in the UK by TJ International, Padstow, Cornwall

Matador is an imprint of Troubador Publishing Ltd

To my muse MJ for continued support, inspiration and belief. Long may it continue.

To Connor Pullen, a gentle giant of a boy whose life was ended far too soon.

And to all of the young people who have expressed their interest, enthusiasm, and encouragement to me in my writing of this book. I hope they will grow up to inspire others by their own writing and imagination.

CHAPTER ONE

Jemma Jessop disappeared today. No one saw her go. She just vanished. One minute she was sitting at her desk in class 9J and the next minute her seat was empty.

Mrs Mulgrew, her teacher, was making adjustments to the written instructions on the whiteboard. She had her back to the pupils, turning around only as the crescendo of talking rose to levels beyond which she was prepared to tolerate.

"Stop that noise, 9J," she called out as she faced the class. "For goodness' sake, why has everyone suddenly decided to talk and shout at the same time? This kind of behaviour is not acceptable. This is a classroom, not some kind of free-for-all market!"

The babble of voices continued.

"SHUSH... BE QUIET EVERYONE!" yelled Mrs Mulgrew.

"Jemma's gone, Miss," cried Amanda.

"What do you mean, Jemma's gone?" asked the teacher, glancing across at the empty desk and chair in the middle of the third row. "Gone where?"

"Don't know, Miss," replied Amanda. "She was there and then she wasn't!"

The noise levels began to rise again as the other pupils all tried to have their say.

"QUIET!" Mrs Mulgrew shouted. "STOP THIS NOISE. I WILL NOT HAVE THIS BEHAVIOUR. NOW WHAT'S going on?" Her voice lowered as silence descended upon the classroom. "Where's Jemma? Her books, pens and bag are still there so she can't be far away. Has she gone to the toilet?"

"She didn't leave the classroom, Miss," piped up Jacob. "I'm sitting right next to the door and I swear that no one has left this room. It's really spooky."

"Nonsense," snorted Mrs Mulgrew, annoyance and impatience now clearly showing in her voice. "Jemma… come on out if you are hiding somewhere. I'm not in the mood for silly games this afternoon."

But Jemma did not appear and after a search beneath all of the desks, a look in the store cupboard, and further interrogation of the pupils whom she suspected of conducting a huge wind-up and practical joke at her expense, Mrs Mulgrew stormed out of the classroom, after first warning 9J of the dire consequences of misbehaviour or noise during her absence, and headed towards the school office.

An hour later Mr and Mrs Jessop, Jemma's parents, sat in the Head's room as he spoke to the police on the telephone.

No one in the school office had seen Jemma leave and she hadn't signed out to say she had gone home early, or been collected by a parent or other adult. Parents said she hadn't gone home nor had she made any contact with them. Film from the CCTV cameras in school did not reveal anyone leaving the school building that afternoon.

A search of every toilet, classroom, corridor, cupboard and storeroom had proved fruitless in locating Jemma, as had a similar search of the sports hall and changing rooms. There was no sign of her anywhere.

The Head had talked to all of Jemma's friends in school and none of them had heard from her. Most hadn't even seen her since lunchtime when they were together in the school yard. There had been no phone calls or text messages from Jemma either, which was very unusual as they were always texting each other, even though they weren't supposed to do so in school. Jemma hadn't replied to any of the latest messages her friends had sent to her and no one was admitting to knowing where she had gone to.

When the policeman and policewoman arrived in school they repeated the searches previously undertaken by school staff.

"Just making sure for our records," said the policeman. "We have to check things out for ourselves."

Jemma's parents were not amused.

"The time it's taken you to do that could have been used in trying to find out where she is *now*," Mr Jessop complained. "Don't you think that if she was anywhere in school someone would have found her by now?" he continued. "What a complete waste of time."

"I'm sorry you feel that way, Sir," replied the police constable, "but we have our own routines so if you wouldn't mind, Sir, we'll need to carry these out and to start with we have to ask you and your wife some questions."

The two constables then proceeded to ask about Jemma's friends and relatives outside of school and about her after-school routines and habits.

"Perhaps she's met up with a friend or gone to visit a relative and forgotten to tell you," said the policeman. "She's a teenager and they don't always think to let people know where they are or what they are doing. I suggest you phone around all of her friends and relatives and see if she's with any of them."

"Does she have a boyfriend?" asked the policewoman. "Maybe she's with him."

"She has no boyfriend," stated Mr Jessop firmly. "Nor would she go anywhere without telling us. Isn't that right, Emily?" He turned his face to look at Mrs Jessop.

"That's right," whispered Emily Jessop, dabbing a paper tissue on the tears that trickled from her eyes and mingled with her mascara, forming dark meandering pathways down her cheeks. "She's a kind and thoughtful girl… A good girl… She tells us everything… This is so unlike our Jemma… Oh please… please… find her… before… before… "

Emily Jessop couldn't bring herself to say what she was thinking. She broke off mid- sentence, giving a great loud sob as she did so.

"So, what are you going to do about finding her?" Mr Jessop asked the policeman.

It was the policewoman who answered first,
"She's only been gone a couple of hours," she reasoned. "We need to check out friends and relatives first. She may be back home soon."

The policeman joined in.

"We'll report the situation to the local police station, along with a description of Jemma, and ask our officers to keep a lookout for her whilst they are out on patrol." He paused.

"And if she doesn't come home, say an hour after the normal time she's supposed to be in, then give us a call and we'll look at the possibility of treating her as a missing person. In the meantime try not to worry too much."

"Is that it?" asked Mr Jessop staring disbelievingly at the constable.

"'Fraid so, Sir," said the constable. "Just go home and check out those friends and relatives, and keep on trying her mobile. I'm sure she'll be all right. As I said, call us later if she doesn't come home when she should."

Emily Jessop let out one last huge sob as she followed her husband out of the head teacher's office.

CHAPTER TWO

"Cherchez la femme," said Detective Inspector Cedric Chalk leaning backwards in his chair, a self-satisfied smile on his lips as he stared smugly across at his subordinate who was busy leafing through a pile of papers.

"Beg pardon, Sir?" replied Detective Sergeant Barry Benson looking up from his rumination.

"Cherchez la femme, Benson," repeated the Detective Inspector. "Have you never heard that before? It's French. It means look for the woman… or the female," he added.

"Yes, Sir, I do know that," said Benson. "But what's the relevance of it now?"

"The relevance, Benson," said DI Chalk triumphantly, "Is that a 15-year-old lad has gone missing from his school and no one has seen or heard from him for three days, so there's every likelihood that he's gone off somewhere with a girl."

"He may not have," argued Benson. "He may have gone off on his own, or with a male friend, or he may have run away from something, had an accident, or even been abducted. It doesn't have to be a girl, Sir. Anything is possible."

"I know anything is possible, Benson," growled Chalk impatiently. "But in my experience when a 15-year-old lad disappears there's usually a lass involved somewhere."

Chalk paused. Gesturing to Benson to move himself he continued. "So go and check out all local missing person lists and see if anyone fits the bill."

Half an hour later DI Chalk sat at his desk looking smugly up at DS Benson.

"What did I tell you, Benson… eh. What did I tell you?" he exclaimed patronisingly. "I knew there was a girl involved and there it is in black and white on one of our own reports."

"We don't know if they're together," argued Benson stubbornly. "We only know that a girl named Jemma Jessop went missing yesterday and no one has heard from her since. They don't even go to the same school, so we don't know if they even know each other."

"There's a link though, isn't there, Benson?" Chalk exulted.

"What's that then, Sir?" asked Benson, not wanting to allow his superior the chance for prolonged gloating.

"Well, they both disappeared from school during the afternoon period, so that has to count for something, doesn't it?" Chalk queried.

"Not quite with you, Sir?" said Benson questioningly.

"Too much of a coincidence for two young people to go missing from school, albeit different schools, within twenty-four hours of each other," reasoned Chalk. "And in any case… I don't believe in coincidences. There's a connection there, you mark my words, Benson. They'll have gone off and set up home together in some campsite or at some bed and breakfast place somewhere on the coast… Love's young dream… Think they're in love and want to be together for ever. I've seen it happen before, Benson. I think we should make a public appeal. Better set up the old national TV interview, eh, Benson? How do I look? Do you think I need make-up?"

"No, Sir," said Benson flatly, resisting an inner urge to make a joke at his senior officer's expense.

CHAPTER THREE

"Where's my daughter?" roared Lanfranco Balconi, storming into the Head's office and disrupting a meeting with school governors.

"I'm sorry but you can't just come barging in here like this. We're having a meeting," began Mr Simcox, the Head, standing up and moving towards the enraged interloper. "If you don't leave I'll have to… "

He didn't get to finish his sentence as Mr Balconi, pushing aside the now empty chairs, grabbed him by his lapels.

"My daughter, Francesca… , where is she?" he demanded. "She didn't come home from school today and none of her friends have seen or heard from her since she went to get her bag at the end of school. Have you kept her behind? Has she got a late detention I haven't been told about? Where is she?"

Mr Balconi was clearly very upset and very angry. Mr Simcox and the governors tried to calm him down and eventually managed to do so before the police arrived, summoned by one of the governors on his mobile phone.

During the next week another twenty-one children mysteriously disappeared from schools in the locality of Cristelee. No one had seen any of them leave and nobody could find anyone who had made contact with any of them once they had gone. It was all very puzzling, almost as if the children had become invisible, or had never existed in the first place.

Police were baffled. DI Chalk's well-composed and well-aired theory of runaway lovers had unravelled as quickly as a woollen jumper caught on a barbed wire fence, but he desperately and defiantly clung on to the last few threads.

"If you look closely, Benson," he reasoned, "you will see that there are an equal number of boys and girls who have gone missing. Now that's gotta mean something, hasn't it? I still think they might be together."

"Are you saying that this is one massive love-in? One big collective lovers' tryst, Sir?" said Benson sceptically. "Or maybe it's a lovers' convention? Or perhaps they are all having a non-stop party somewhere?"

"Don't get sarcastic, Benson," growled Chalk. "I'm merely suggesting that there's more to this than meets the eye in as much as equal numbers brings us back to coincidences and you know what I think of coincidences don't you, Benson?"

Benson remained silent as Chalk continued with his wild speculations.

"Perhaps there's a new cult forming somewhere, maybe some fanatic is contacting young people by text or internet and inviting them to join him, or her, on a mountain top somewhere in preparation for the end of the world. Or perhaps someone is forming a gang to go shoplifting and stealing, a bit like a modern-day Fagin."

"Maybe, Sir," agreed Benson, fighting hard to resist the urge to laugh out loud at his boss's far-fetched hypotheses.

Chalk fixed him with a stony stare. "Or maybe it's something altogether more sinister and dangerous," he concluded.

Over the next two weeks ten of the missing children reappeared. Jemma turned up in her bedroom, Francesca was found in the local library, whilst others appeared in a variety of situations including a supermarket, a games warehouse and a police station.

Not one of the children could remember anything that had happened to them, nor did they have any recollection of where they had been. Strangely, none of them could remember much about their friends or their own recent life experiences. It was as if their short-term memories had been wiped clean.

Another disturbing feature that was common to all of the children was that they all seemed to have undergone a major change in personality.

Before their disappearance each child had been described as bubbly, bright, friendly and caring and every one of them had been kind and helpful. All were popular and had lots of friends and all had enjoyed good relationships with parents, brothers and sisters.

Since returning each child had become grumpy, angry, loud, complaining, uncaring and unhappy.

Now in school each child spent their time arguing with teachers, neglecting school and home work, and picking on other children and bullying them. They were no different at home as they got into lots of arguments with parents, refused to do whatever it was they were asked and spent a lot of time alone in their rooms.

"There's nothing to worry about. It's probably only temporary," said an Educational Psychologist who had spoken to all of the children. "I think you'll find that its delayed shock brought about by the trauma of whatever has happened to them. I think they are probably stressed out and this causes them to behave in this way. It is very unusual for anyone to completely change their personality from good to bad in this way so I don't think we need get too concerned at this stage. Once the children have got back into their regular routines with the people they know and care about, at home and in school, I think you will find that they will become less stressed and traumatised and then they will get back to being themselves again."

A lot of people hoped the Psychologist was right.

Meanwhile ten more children disappeared from different schools in the next few days. The pattern was always the same: they would disappear during the school day from wherever they happened to be at the time, whether in their classroom, on the sports field or in the sports hall. Children would suddenly disappear from corridors, drama studios, science labs, even toilets. No one ever saw them go, they just went. One child was playing in a football match and was only missed when a soft back pass trickled into the unguarded goal that the child was supposed to be minding.

Sometimes a child would go when they were with a friend, who may have been talking to them at the time. But the friend never saw them go, only realising they weren't there when they failed to answer a question or join in the conversation. It was all very strange and although lots of people had ideas, no one really knew what was happening.

The local newspapers, radio and TV were having a field day. They could always find someone willing enough to offer some outlandish and extravagant theory about what they thought was the cause of this phenomenon.

"ALIENS ABDUCT CHILDREN TO EXPERIMENT ON THEM!" screamed one headline in the local evening newspaper. The story went on to give several so-called eyewitness accounts of coloured lights in the sky and disc and cigar-shaped flying objects silently gliding through the night skies above local parks and housing estates, before concluding with the idea that children were being abducted and tested as a prelude to some kind of alien invasion.

Other stories and theories appeared with incredible regularity as local people, many of whom were in well-respected jobs and positions in the community and certainly should have known better, queued up to be interviewed and to articulate their own particular theory.

Every day a new idea was put forward and published in the paper or portrayed on news programmes. The theories included mass hypnosis, telepathic communication with the intent of preparing children for a major evacuation of the planet, devil worship, secret cults and societies, a government plot to control and brainwash children to prevent them from becoming dissenting and disagreeable adults, and scientists kidnapping children to conduct brain cell swaps with aggressive and uncommunicative baboons and chimpanzees.

It seemed as if everyone had an idea that they believed in, however ridiculous and far-fetched it was, and like all things unknown and unexplained, the more absurd and crazy the idea the more people were inclined to believe it.

Every day there would be some official from the police, from the education department, some local councillor, or parent, or just some ordinary member of the public, appearing on the radio or TV news to express their views and opinions on events and what should be done. But nobody actually did anything. For a start no one knew what to do, and secondly no-one really had any idea of why or how these children were managing to disappear and then reappear some days later recognisable only in physical appearance, as their demeanour and behaviour had changed drastically.

The police, like everyone else, were baffled too, but DI Chalk still stuck to at least part of his original beliefs.

"I'm telling you, Benson," he said emphatically, "there's either a new cult developing or these youngsters are having some sort of boy/girl relationships on a large scale that probably involves some kind of hallucinogenic drug that triggers off amnesia and causes their personality to change for the worse."

"How would that work then, Sir?" asked Benson dubiously.

"I don't know. I'm a detective not a doctor!" snapped Chalk, his exasperation clearly showing. "But there are drugs that change people's personality and bring about aggressive and negative behaviour. Side effects... Yes, that's what they call them... side effects. That's what we should be looking at, Benson... new drugs coming on to the market, never mind blooming aliens and unidentified flying objects. You check out the side effects of all of the so-called recreational drugs, Benson, and let me know if any fit this pattern."

"With all due respect, Sir," argued Benson, "the young people who are disappearing don't seem to be the type I'd say were likely to be involved in drugs. Parents, friends *and* teachers all say they are really likeable, helpful, kind and well-adjusted young people. So I'd say we're barking up the wrong tree here, Sir, if we think that drugs play any part in this."

"Have you got a better idea?" barked Chalk.

"Well... no, Sir,... not at this precise moment in time," Benson replied. "But the fact that I don't have another theory doesn't necessarily mean that yours is right either."

"So we do nothing then, Benson?" Chalk queried, before adding sarcastically, "I'm sure the Superintendent will be delighted to hear that. So when he asks me what progress we are making with the missing children I'll just tell him that Benson says we do nothing as he doesn't have any ideas and that means that everyone else's ideas are wrong too, eh?"

"That's not what I meant, Sir," said Benson, feeling a little miffed that his colleague had put him down like that. "I just meant that there could be any number of possible explanations for what is happening, as I've said to you before." He paused. "And we don't know anything for certain. But if you think drugs might be involved then I'll do as you ask and get it checked out."

"Then get on with it," barked Chalk. "Go and check out the points I've asked you to, and stop trying to find ways to avoid the obvious. I've been in this job a long time, Benson... a lot longer than you... so instead of standing around bleating that we don't know anything, go and find something... and just as a matter of interest we do know something and that's why I've asked you to check out the side effects of drugs, so we can eliminate them from our enquiries if nothing fits."

Chalk sighed and gave a half smile in Benson's direction. "We'll make a detective out of you yet, Benson," he said.

Benson stared balefully at his boss before returning the half smile. He shrugged his shoulders, turned and walked out of the office, closing the door noisily as he did so.

Later that day as he sat at his own desk checking out the internet for information on what he considered to be "his DI's ridiculous ideas", Benson resolved that he, unlike his boss, would keep an open mind in his own bid to find the real cause of the disappearances and the changes in personality that were happening to children in local schools.

CHAPTER FOUR

At Hoblues High School, the after-school CAB group were in session. CAB stood for "Children Against Bullying", and the group consisted of a number of pupils who wanted to make a stand against bullying and highlight the effects it had on victims.

The group met weekly, after school, and prepared school assemblies and produced plays, stories, poems and posters with an anti-bullying theme. They then shared their productions with the rest of the school pupils and staff.

CAB was a popular group with a lot of active members many of whom were now in the classroom logging on to computers as they prepared for whatever it was they were going to do that evening. The pupils laughed and chatted amongst themselves as they worked. The atmosphere within the group was friendly and cheerful and the two members of the school staff, Tom Nilson and Rob Chatel, who ran the group were able to relax and share the informality of the situation with the pupils. Everyone was having a good time.

Suddenly the conviviality of the classroom was shattered by the sound of a loud and very piercing scream!

Mr Nilson immediately rushed across to the children sitting at the table from where the scream had emanated.

"Amy?" he asked. "What on earth is the matter?"

Amy sat shaking. Her hand was visibly trembling as she pointed at the empty chair next to her.

"It's Ella," she said in a cracked voice. "She's just disappeared!… Honestly, Mr Nilson, she was sitting there making a poster on the computer and we were talking about a party we're going to at the weekend, then she's gone… just gone… vanished… you know, like in one of those sci-fi films on the telly where they make people disappear in a flash… except there was no flash here… but I still saw it… Well, not exactly saw it but you know, I saw her go… I was looking at her as she was talking and she sort of shimmered and then faded away… Oh Sir, what's happening?… Where's she gone?"

Amy started crying as the other group members gathered around her. They all started talking rapidly and excitedly about what Amy had just told Mr Nilson.

The two teachers managed to maintain an element of calm within the group and Mr Nilson asked if anyone else had witnessed the event just described by Amy.

There was a lot of head shaking and voices loudly expressing a negative answer, but amid the noes came a thought-provoking observation from Lucy.

"I didn't actually see Ella disappear," she stated. "But I swear that as I looked across at Amy, just as she screamed, I caught a flash of movement in the corner of her computer screen. It was only a flash and only for a moment, like it was there and then it was gone, but I definitely saw something."

Lucy hesitated, her face pink and flushed.

"You'll probably think I'm stupid or mad or seeing things but it looked like… " She stopped. "Oh nothing… forget it, maybe I was seeing things in the excitement of the moment."

"No, go on, Lucy," said Mr Nilson. "We don't think you're stupid or mad. What was it? What do you think you saw in the computer?"

"It looked like it was a tiny person," whispered Lucy, trying to avoid looking at anyone.

"Are you sure that's what it looked like?" asked Mr Chatel. Lucy nodded.

"Can you describe what this tiny person looked like?" Mr Chatel continued.

"Not really," said Lucy. "Like I said it was only for a split second so I didn't get much more than a quick glance… but I'm sure it was a person and I'm pretty sure it had its mouth open as if shouting or screaming."

Lucy thought for a moment and added, "I know this sounds ridiculous but the figure also appeared to be banging on the glass at the front of the computer screen… like it was trapped and trying to get out."

"Trick of the light," denounced DI Chalk. "Probably an overactive imagination influenced by reading or watching too many mysteries and adventure programmes on TV. She hears a scream, gets scared, looks quickly across at where it's coming from, catches a glimpse of the computer screen which has on it a video from You Tube or something, and thinks it's some tiny person trapped in the screen. Classic example of a young girl's mind being influenced by a scary event and opening up her fears, and the rest is down to her vivid imagination."

Chalk and Benson had just got back from a visit to Hoblues School, where they had chatted with Lucy and Amy and the rest of the CAB group members.

"There might be something in it, Sir," contradicted Benson, feeling a bit annoyed that his boss was dismissing the children's statements so lightly. "Maybe we ought to follow it up?"

"And do what?" asked Chalk scathingly. "Open up every computer to see if there are little people living in there? You'll be telling me next that you believe in fairies, leprechauns and little green men. For goodness' sake, Benson, think about it... How on earth could what the girl saw be anything other than imagination, illusion, or a video or advert on the internet? We need to concentrate on the girl... What's her name?... Ella... that's our focus. She's disappeared, like all of the others. It's the first disappearance in this school so what does that mean?"

Chalk proceeded to answer his own question. "Whatever is causing this is spreading. We've now got a new school involved and that's worrying. If it follows the pattern of the other schools then more children will go from Hoblues so I concede that we might have to concentrate on them a bit, but not on some dreamt-up little elf supposedly seen in a computer by a young girl who was probably hysterical, or something similar, because she'd just heard another girl screaming out loud and as a result let her own imagination run away with her. Get a grip, Benson!"

Ella Pollet felt a bit woozy. It wasn't a pain. It wasn't a feeling like wanting to be sick. It was a peculiar feeling, one she couldn't remember ever having experienced before. The sensation she felt was strange, almost ethereal. She felt unreal, as if she didn't exist, as if she was floating and flying at the same time.

Ella stared hard at the computer screen in front of her. She made a concerted effort to focus and concentrate on the work she was doing, trying to imagine what her poster would look like when it was finished.

"Come on, keep your mind on what you are doing," she urged herself. "Don't think about how you are feeling. If you forget about it then it might go away. Talk to someone."

Ella turned to Amy and began chatting about the party at the weekend. It was Bethany's birthday and everyone in their friendship group was going. Ella had been really excited as it was the first party she had been to in ages and she was looking forward to the weekend.

As she was talking to Amy, Ella screwed up her face and tried hard to shut out the weird feelings and thoughts that seemed to be taking over her brain. She looked around the room where she could see all of her friends laughing and chatting away as usual.

"What are you wearing for the party on Saturday?" she asked Amy, in a last-ditch effort to hold on to reality. But she never got an answer as her hold on the real world diminished with increasing rapidity.

The feeling was now so strong that Ella couldn't resist it any longer. She closed her eyes and then quickly opened them again as she made one last effort to save herself. Then she was flying. Well, at least that's how it seemed. To her great alarm Ella found she was shrinking too! Either that or everyone and everything else in the room were getting bigger!

Ella could see her friends, her desk and her computer growing larger and larger before her eyes. She gasped loudly as she suddenly felt herself being propelled at great speed towards her computer screen. Ella tried to scream but no sound came from her lips. She tried to grab on to something to stop herself. But everything was now so much bigger than she was so her hands were too small to get a grip on anything. Her hands flailed wildly as she tumbled through the now seemingly massive space between her desk and her computer screen.

With all hope lost Ella braced herself for the impact. The computer screen loomed large in front of her as she continued her rapid descent towards it at a considerable rate of knots. She closed her eyes again and tried to imagine what the pain would be like when she hit the screen at speed. She didn't doubt that it would hurt, probably a lot, given that she was now quite tiny and the screen was huge and made of what seemed like solid glass.

Ella was very scared.

"I'm going to die," she said to herself. "I'm going to hit my head on that glass screen and the glass is going to stay put but my head is going to shatter!"

Ella began to cry. "Oh please help me," she mouthed to no one in particular. "Please... please help me... I don't want to die!"

But there was no impact! Ella's hurtling body hit the screen full pelt... and came out on the other side! She was inside the computer screen. She could see out, just as if it was a window. She could still see her friends. She could also see Mr Nilson and Mr Chatel. They appeared to be concerned about something and Amy was pointing at the chair that Ella had been sitting on.

Ella tried to wave and call out. She tried knocking on the glass, but her limbs felt as if they were being controlled by some force that didn't allow her to move them freely, as she wanted to. What's more, her voice seemed to have disappeared.

A split second later, although it seemed much longer, Ella could no longer see out of the screen, even though she was still behind the glass. The computer screen, towering above her, was now blank and dark.

"A bit like those tinted windows you get on expensive limousines carrying famous people," Ella thought to herself, for no other reason than to try to keep her sanity.

She was scared. She didn't know what to do next. So, heart beating loudly and madly, Ella sat down and waited for whatever it was that had brought her to this unimaginable and scary place to put in an appearance.

CHAPTER FIVE

Back in the classroom Mr Nilson and Mr Chatel were desperately trying to calm the children, but it wasn't easy. Everyone wanted to talk about Ella's disappearance. What's more, everyone was scared and worried that they might be the next to go. After all they had all read about, or seen on the local news, stories of children disappearing in another part of the town, and now it seemed to be happening here too, in this school. The one that they all came to each weekday, and were sitting in now.

Mr Nilson announced that he was going to let the Head know what had happened, and he left the room, hotly pursued by Amy, Lucy and Elizabeth who were still trying to understand what had just taken place in the classroom.

"Do you think Ella will be all right, Sir?" asked Elizabeth, anxiety showing in her voice. "I mean… how could she just vanish like that in a classroom full of people? What do you think has happened to her, Sir? Where do you think she's gone?… Where do you think she is?… And what about her parents?… What are they gonna say?"

"Mr Nilson, what about the figure I saw in the computer?" Lucy chipped in "Do you think that was Ella?… Do you think she's inside the computer?… Or do you think that it was the figure in the computer that made Ella disappear?"

"I've no idea where Ella has gone or how it happened," answered Mr Nilson, trying to keep his voice calm and unflustered in order not to panic the girls even more. "We need to let Mrs Stewber know what's happened so that she can decide what to do next. That's where I'm off to now so please, girls, go back into the classroom and stay with Mr Chatel whilst I do that, thank you."

Amy, Lucy and Elizabeth went back into class as requested as Mr Nilson knocked on the Head's door.

An hour or so later DI Chalk addressed the small group of people sitting in Mrs Stewber's office.

"I have to tell you," he began, in his most serious tone, "this is not an uncommon occurrence in this area of late, as you will know if you've been following the news. However… " Chalk drew a deep breath and continued. "It's the first time we've had a disappearance in this school… and in this particular area of Cristelee… So I think it's obvious that whatever is causing this is spreading."

"Oh go on… state the obvious… say what everybody already knows, why don't you?" thought Benson, his face etched in irritation as he watched his superior officer. "That isn't what they want to hear. The parents want to know what's happened to their daughter and what we are going to do about finding her."

Ella's parents stared at DI Chalk as he spoke. Along with everyone else in the room they waited eagerly for him to continue, but Chalk gave a short cough, turned quickly and walked over to sit next to DC Benson.

"What are the police doing about Ella's disappearance?" her father asked. "Are there any clues?"

"Do you have any ideas about where she might be?" Ella's mother added, her face filled with anxiety and worry. "What about the others who went missing and then came back?… Where had they been?"

Chalk gave another little cough, which he tried to stifle with his hand, before answering.

"We don't really know," he croaked in a quiet voice. "But we do know she will be back within a week if this takes the same form as all of the other missing children. The pattern in all of the other cases is that they turn up about a week after they disappear. So I guess we will just have to be patient and hope that Ella might be able to remember something that will give us a clue as to where she is, and who is doing this, when she returns."

"Is that all?" screamed Mrs Pollet, Ella's mother. "My baby goes missing and all you can say is wait until she comes back in a week or so and hope she can remember where she's been? What are we supposed to do in the meantime? Our daughter has disappeared and she's not the first either. You're the police… you're supposed to protect people… you're supposed to solve crimes… why aren't you doing something?"

"We are trying, Ma'am," stuttered Chalk apologetically, his composure evaporating under the verbal attack from Ella's mother. "But to tell you the truth, so many children are going missing and then returning without anyone knowing what's happened or remembering anything about where they've been or who they've seen, or even remembering going in the first place, that we are struggling. We have no information about what's going on."

Chalk coughed again, then continued. "I can't tell you anything as yet but I can say that we have some ideas… don't we, Benson?"

Chalk turned to Benson for some relief, with a look that pleaded for his subordinate to bale him out of the mess he was getting himself into.

"Yes Sir, we do," said Benson, who was quite enjoying seeing Chalk being given a hard time by Ella's parents.

Chalk stared at Benson and motioned for him to continue, but Benson had said all he was going to say in these circumstances. He didn't want the parents turning on him and asking him awkward questions that he couldn't find an answer to. So Chalk was forced to carry on talking.

"I can't tell you exactly what these ideas are though as it may jeopardise or complicate the situation, but we are following them up and we will let you know if we come up with anything positive."

Chalk was starting to sweat, even though it was quite cool in the Head's room. He coughed once more and then said, "I think you should go home now and leave it to us. I'm sure your daughter will be home soon and you can call when she returns so we can come and interview her, just in case she does happen to remember anything that might be useful to us."

"Ella," said Mrs Pollet. "Her name is Ella. Don't keep on referring to her as 'she' or 'your daughter', her name is Ella."

Mrs Pollet paused and then giving Chalk a withering look said, "Oh, by the way… Thanks for nothing!"

Back in the police station Chalk sat at his desk in his office. He rubbed his hands across his face and screwed up his eyes.

"What on earth is happening, Benson?" he sighed. "Why aren't we getting any clues or any leads?"

"Not sure, Sir," Benson responded limply. It had been a long day and he was feeling tired. All he wanted to do at this moment was to go home and get some sleep. He had no desire to sit and listen to his boss and his theories again, but Chalk wasn't to be put off so easily.

"Over fifty children have gone missing so far, Benson, and no one can give us any clue as to why they disappear and what happens to them whilst they are away. Everyone comes back, but when they do they have all become aggressive, argumentative bullies. The complete opposite to what they were before they vanished. Why?… Come on, Benson… think… who… or what… is doing this?"

Chalk stroked his chin and then stood up, his expression suddenly brighter.

"You know… I still think this has got something to do with a cult or with drugs," he mused. He looked up at Benson and added, "Perhaps both. Anyway I'm sure it will keep until morning. Come on, Benson, let's go home."

CHAPTER SIX

Ella did come back during the next week. She was spotted, in the laptop department of a local electrical dealer's shop, by Amy.

"Hi, Ella... Ella" called out Amy, rushing over to talk to her friend.

Ella looked at Amy.

"Who are *you* and why are you looking at me like that?" she asked aggressively.

"Ella, it's me... Amy," said Amy, puzzled by her friend's response.

"Amy?" questioned Ella. "I don't know any Amy, so why don't you just bog off and leave me alone, you squinty-eyed little creep."

Amy reeled under the verbal abuse that came her way from the mouth of her lifelong pal. She could feel the tears welling up in her eyes, but she forced herself to hold them back. This was her friend, who had been missing for a week. Everyone had been searching for her, and everyone had been missing her, Amy especially, and now here she was in a local store, pretending she didn't know the person who had been her best friend since they were both toddlers at play school.

"Ella... Why are you acting this way?" asked Amy, her voice trembling as she fought back her tears. "Where have you been? What's happened to you? When did you get back?"

"Look, I'll not tell you again," growled Ella, thrusting her now contorted face into Amy's. "I don't know you… and what's more I'm not your friend Ella, and I've not been anywhere." She breathed in deeply. "And… if you say anything else to me I'll put my fist straight down your throat, you sad, pathetic, ugly little weasel."

This time Amy couldn't stop the tears. They poured down her cheeks as she pulled away from Ella and ran across the store. She rushed headlong to where her mum was checking out the latest iPads.

"Amy? What on earth is the matter?" asked her mum. "Why are you crying? Have you hurt yourself?"

"Oh Mum, it was horrible," cried Amy. "I saw Ella… over there". She pointed to where Ella was. There was no one there except for a man in a pinstripe suit, and a young couple looking at the laptops on display.

"Are you sure, dear?" asked Mum. "I would have thought that would have made you happy, not leave you crying like this."

"It would have, but when I went up to her and spoke to her, she said she wasn't Ella and then she was really nasty to me, calling me names and threatening to hit me. I was scared, Mum, really scared!"

"Well, she's not there now, Amy love, and as you and Ella are such good friends I would be very surprised if she'd reacted like that towards you if it really was Ella. You probably made a mistake and just thought it was Ella as you're missing her and thinking about her all of the time lately, and it was just someone who looked like Ella."

"But I know Ella, Mum, and I swear it was her," sobbed Amy. "Why did she treat me like that and say such horrible things to me?"

"Oh, Amy," said her Mum gently as she hugged her daughter tightly. "I think you got it wrong and just happened to talk to someone who was perhaps in a bad mood already and when you called her Ella she got angry and so was very rude and nasty. Whoever it was she's gone now so she can't hurt you. Anyway you're with me and I won't let anyone hurt you. You're safe here. Now, here's a tissue, dry your eyes and we'll go and get something to eat and drink, eh?"

Amy nodded and took the tissue. She gave a good blow, wiped her eyes and nose, hooked her arm into her mother's arm and they both walked off to find some food.

Next day at school everyone was talking about Ella's return. Apparently she had been seen by several pupils and her parents had phoned Mrs Stewber to say she was home but wouldn't be in school for some time as she wasn't herself, and also the police needed to speak with her.

Amy told her friends in the CAB group about what had happened yesterday when she saw Ella in the store.

"I saw her yesterday too," said Janie. "She was standing on the corner of the street where she lives and looking around at all of the houses as if she couldn't remember which one was hers. I said hello to her and asked her how she was and where she'd been."

"What happened?" asked Amy.

"She told me to get lost and mind my own business," Janie replied. "I told her that if she wanted to act like that then she could find someone else to hang out with."

"It's very strange though isn't it?" said Zoe. "You know... her going missing and then coming back and not seeming to know where she lives or to know any of her friends."

"Yes," answered Simran. "And to be so horrible to people she knows. That's not like Ella. She was never nasty to anyone whether she knew them or not."

"I think this must have something to do with her being away," said Courtney. "Do you think we ought to tell the police about it?"

"They will probably have spoken with Ella already," piped up Amir. "I bet they know she's denying who she is and I wouldn't be surprised if Ella's been nasty to them too, especially if they ask her lots of questions."

"I think we *should* tell them," said Janie. "They need all the information they can get hold of so they can find out what's happened, and I'm sure they would like to know about how much Ella has changed while she's been away. I think it's important for them to know."

"Yeah," drawled Zoe sarcastically. "*SO* important. What are they gonna do with that little bit of useless knowledge? They won't do anything with it. Look at when they came to talk to us when Ella disappeared. They sure took Amy seriously when she told them about seeing a figure in the computer, didn't they? Did you hear that Chalk bloke? He practically called Amy a liar *and* he hinted that he thought she was going doolally. Get real, Janie, why would they be interested in what we tell them now?"

"We *do* need to help Ella though," said Amy earnestly, jumping in quickly as she saw Janie's face fall at Zoe's scornful remarks. "The girl I saw yesterday had Ella's body and looks but she didn't have Ella's personality. There's something very strange happening here. How can someone go missing… No, on second thoughts Ella didn't actually go missing… let's face it… she disappeared… right in front of our eyes… we all saw it… she disappeared."

"Well, we didn't actually see her go" said Daniel jokingly. Then he saw the looks the others were giving him and hastily added, "But we all know what you mean, Amy, and we *were* all there when it happened."

"So what *do* you think happened to Ella?" asked Zoe. "How is it possible for someone to just disappear in a room full of people?… And in a school too… And what about Lucy's figure in the computer? Who or what was that?"

"This is a real mystery just like you see in films or on TV," Janie interjected, perking up a little after her earlier rebuff by Zoe. She gave a little involuntary shudder as she spoke. "Does anybody else find it scary? I do… I mean, does anyone think that if it can happen to Ella it can happen to someone else too? I suppose it could happen to any one of us!"

There was a long silence after Janie spoke, as everyone mused over what she had just said. It was true and although everyone had asked themselves the same question at some time in the past week, no one had actually been brave enough to answer it or to say it out loud. Now Janie had done so it could no longer be ignored.

"Do you really think that one of us could disappear too?" Elizabeth's voice carried the anxiety that everyone was now feeling.

"Well, we know that pupils have gone from other schools and that those events have involved a number of pupils over a period of time, so now it's started in Hoblues I guess there'll be more to come," said Daniel glumly.

"And how do you know that, Dan?" asked Zoe.

"I've been watching the news and reading the papers," Daniel replied. "This has been going on for a few months now and whoever or whatever is taking those children always takes several children from the same school."

"So perhaps we *should* tell the police what we know?" asked Janie hopefully. She was a little worried about the direction in which this conversation was going.

"No," said Zoe emphatically. "We have nothing to tell them other than a couple of us have seen Ella and she's been horrible and nasty. Can you imagine what Chalk will say if we tell him Ella has been rude to Amy? How's that gonna help?"

"We should do something, though" said Daniel. "I don't want to be next and end up like Ella."

A chorus of "Nor me" and "Me neither" followed his words as everyone thought of what Daniel had said.

"But what *can* we do?" asked Elizabeth. "It's not like we know everything that's happening or that we are the police… or even adults. We don't have any clout. Who will take notice of us?"

"I think there is something we can do," said Amy, screwing up her brow in thought. "But we all have to do this, not just one or two of us, in order for it to have any chance of working. No one can drop out."

"Okay," enthused Zoe. "Tell us what you're thinking. What is this thing that we all have to sign up to?"

"Well," Amy began. There was complete silence as everyone strained to hear what Amy was proposing.

"We've all agreed that it's quite likely that someone else will disappear from Hoblues and that there's a chance it will be one of us, given that Ella disappeared from a CAB session after school. It could be something to do with the timing and if so then it makes it more likely it *will* happen again in one of these sessions. Do you agree?"

Everyone nodded and mouthed their yeses.

"So what are you suggesting we do?" asked Zoe.

"It's only an idea and I haven't had time to think it through properly yet, but what if every one of us had some kind of device that helped us keep in contact with each other all of the time, so if someone disappeared they could let the others know what was going on?"

Amy looked around the group expectantly.

"Mobile phone," shouted Daniel. "We could use our mobile phones."

"Not really," said Courtney. "Firstly we aren't allowed to have them switched on when we are in school, and secondly what if there's no signal for the person who disappears? How are they going to keep in touch with the others if that happens?"

There was a collective sigh of disappointment at Courtney's comments.

"We don't know for certain that there won't be a signal," said Daniel, countering Courtney's comments with his own assertion.

Courtney responded with similar authority.

"I didn't say definitely that they wouldn't get a signal. I said they *might* not get a signal," she said forcefully.

"How do you know that?" asked Daniel brusquely.

"I don't," said Courtney impatiently. "Which is why I said *might* and not *won't*. I'm just guessing, I suppose, because no one has used their phone when they've been taken and I was thinking that maybe they would have if there'd been a signal."

"Maybe they didn't get the chance," said Simran quietly, shivering instinctively at the thought of something stopping Ella from using her phone.

"OK," said Courtney sharply. "Maybe they didn't, but we still can't assume that there will be a signal so we need to look at alternatives."

"All right" said Daniel. "No need to get so prickly about it."

Courtney was about to reply when Zoe intervened.

"Cool it, you two. This isn't helping. We need to look at other options."

"So what else can we use?" Daniel raised the question, before delivering his own verdict on what he saw as an

34

ill-conceived strategy. "That's stuffed Amy's plan before we've even got started."

"Sorry," said Amy despondently. "I told you I hadn't properly thought it through."

"So we just forget about it and wait until one of us disappears, is that it?" wailed Ruby. "I don't mind telling you, I'm scared, I really am."

"No, we don't forget it," Zoe stated defiantly. "Maybe we can't use our phones but there must be something else we can use. Amy, it's a good plan. We just need to think about how we can carry it out. Anyone got any thoughts?"

"We could ask Mr Nilson and Mr Chatel for help," said Janie.

"Yes, we could," replied Zoe, glaring at Janie once more. "And then what do we say when they ask us why we want to find something that we can hold or wear that keeps us in contact with each other when they both know we all have mobiles and that we use these all the time we want to talk or text?"

"We tell them the truth," ventured Janie.

"No we don't," said Zoe firmly. "They may be okay but they are still teachers, and as such they won't let us do this. They won't let us take the risk. They'll have to stop us... and tell our parents too. That won't help us one bit and we'll never be able to find out the truth about Ella's disappearance."

"Oh," Janie sighed, "I suppose so... sorry... I wasn't thinking... I was just trying to help."

"Yeah, OK," said Zoe soothingly.

"Let's look on the internet," Daniel suggested. "We can look at miniature communication devices... you know, like the police and secret service sometimes use. I've seen them in spy films. There must be some way of buying something like that."

"Do that then, Dan," said Zoe. "But do it at home, not here. We don't want any of the staff finding out what you are looking at and asking questions about it. Remember, since Ella's disappearance everyone is on the lookout for anything unusual, and everyone is full of suspicion."

"OK" agreed Daniel, "point taken. I'll do it on my laptop in my bedroom."

"What about us trying to find out more about the other people who went missing?" Courtney asked.

"How will that help?" Daniel questioned.

"Well, we could see if there are any particular things they have in common with each other. Maybe that will give us a clue as to whether any of us have similar things that might make us targets. We might be able to predict who could be the next to go and perhaps come up with something that could help us stop it."

Courtney looked around to see if the reaction of the others was favourable, and seeing supportive nods from some she felt brave enough to conclude, "Or there might be a pattern, such as the time of disappearance or when or where they came back. Anything really that might help us."

"That sounds like a reasonable idea," Zoe concurred. "But how will you go about it?"

"I hadn't really thought," answered Courtney. "I just got the thought in my head… but I suppose I could try to look at old newspaper reports on each of the disappearances. I guess I'll be able to find some on the internet. It'll be a start."

"Good, you do that," Zoe enthused. "But as I said to Dan, don't do it here. Have you got a computer at home?"

Courtney nodded.

"Then go for it," said Zoe.

CHAPTER SEVEN

Ella sat on the settee in her front room, alongside her parents. Her face was dark and sullen as she flashed a hostile glare at DI Chalk and DS Benson, who sat in the easy chairs opposite.

"Now, Ella," Chalk began. "We know it's been a difficult week for you… and for your parents," he added hastily as he remembered their previous hostility towards him at their last meeting. He nodded his acknowledgement of Mr and Mrs Pollet, before carrying on his conversation with Ella. "We also know that you probably don't feel like talking about it but we have to ask you some questions. Can you tell us anything about what happened to you?"

Ella just stared ahead and shrugged her shoulders. Mr and Mrs Pollet exchanged glances that were a combination of embarrassment and exasperation as they silently willed their daughter to tell all. Both parents looked tired and drawn and Mrs Pollet in particular looked as if she hadn't slept for some time. Mr Pollet's face yielded a glimpse of eyes that were obviously finding great difficulty in believing that what Ella was displaying was anything other than teenage tantrums and defiance. His jaw was set in what could only be described as anger.

Chalk broke the increasing silence.

"Any little thing you can remember at all, Ella," he ventured. "However small or insignificant it might seem to you, it may help us find out who is doing this."

Chalk's pleas again met with silence as Ella carried on staring at the two detectives without saying a word.

"Ella love, come on, try to remember," encouraged Mrs Pollet softly, as she leaned forward and took Ella's hand in hers. "They're not here to have a go at you. They're just trying to do their job and find out who is doing this terrible thing."

Ella's lips tightened even more. She gave a scornful look in her mother's direction as she vigorously snatched her hand away from Mrs Pollet's supportive grip.

"Ella, don't be so rude!" shouted Mr Pollet. "We're all trying to help you but all you do is throw it back in our faces. I'm sick of you behaving like this. Now answer the questions and be done with it!"

"David... please," said Mrs Pollet wearily. "You know she doesn't respond to shouting."

"Strikes me she doesn't respond to anything since she came back," said Mr Pollet angrily. He turned to Chalk. "She's been like this ever since she returned to us. Either stony silence, or rage, or anger and open defiance. She's not the Ella we remember. She's changed... and not for the better."

Mrs Pollet chipped in. "Ella was such a lovely girl, so helpful, kind and considerate. She would do anything for anyone and she was so well liked. In fact she was a pleasure to be with and we loved spending time with her. We did lots of things together as a family, went to the cinema, went shopping, went out for meals, played games, watched TV, laughed... "

Mrs Pollet's voiced trailed off. She looked despairingly towards Ella, who had shown no sign of emotion or recognition during her mother's statement.

"Now look at her," Mrs Pollet continued. "She's turned into a sullen, angry, argumentative child who won't talk except to shout at us or criticise us, and she won't do a thing around the house. You should see her bedroom, it's a disgrace. This is not our Ella. What's happened to her? Where's my lovely, lovely daughter?"

Mrs Pollet started to cry as she finished. Mr Pollet moved across to comfort his wife but Ella remained unmoved.

Chalk shook his head slowly.

"I'm afraid I don't know the answer to that, Mrs Pollet," he concluded.

Benson watched this scenario without saying a word. He was thinking about Ella and how Mrs Pollet had just described her behaviour in the past week. To be honest he found it hard to get beyond the thought in his head that the behaviour she had just illustrated was about par for the course and could be ascribed to thousands of teenagers across the length and breadth of the country, and at any time, never mind the past week. At least that was his experience and he should know as the father of two teenage boys.

Benson looked at Ella, who appeared to be totally oblivious and uncaring about what was happening around her. He suddenly felt very sorry for her parents who were quite evidently finding it very hard to come to terms with what had happened to the daughter they had so clearly doted upon. He felt a bit of a lump in his throat as he took in the scene. There was something desperately sad about watching two parents becoming distraught and angry as they fell apart in front of two strangers, whilst the object of their feelings, a child who they so obviously cared about and loved, sat zombie-like next to them on their settee.

"How difficult it must be for them to cope," Benson thought. "What must it be like to have your child go missing and to go through the agonies of that loss, finding it replaced, seven days later, by the joy of finding her again, only to suffer an even greater loss as you discover how she has changed, resulting in you having her near you but being unable to talk with her or to recognise her as your daughter. It's like having a stranger take over your home. I wonder how I'd cope if it was one of my children?"

"Do you take drugs, Ella?"

The question jolted Benson back to reality. He stared disbelievingly at Chalk who had posed it.

"What on earth did he ask that for?" Benson asked himself. "It's the wrong question to ask, and in any case she is never going to admit to taking drugs in front of her parents and two policemen, even if she was an addict and in full control of her memory and her mind."

Ella didn't respond. She stared at Chalk, looking right through him. It was her father who broke the silence.

"Of course she doesn't take drugs," Mr Pollet snapped. "What a stupid question to ask. We've already told you what a lovely, responsible and respectful child Ella was before all of this happened. What have drugs got to do with anything? Is that what you think caused the changes in her? Do you seriously think that even if someone had forced Ella to take drugs for the whole of the week she was away, this would have changed her entire personality this much? More likely it would have made her severely ill or possibly killed her, but it wouldn't permanently affect her this much in a week."

"Drugs do change people's personality, Sir" said Chalk. "Sadly Benson and I see this quite often in our work."

"That may be so, Detective Inspector," argued Mr Pollet, scathingly, before adding, "But you must be aware that such extreme changes are unlikely to occur in just one week?"

"We can't say for certain, Sir," stated Chalk pompously.

"Yes, we can," retorted Mr Pollet. "I'm a Medical Consultant so I think I know what I'm talking about. You're barking up the wrong tree if you think drugs are responsible for this, Detective Inspector. You should be looking for other explanations."

"What about friends?" asked a now flustered Chalk, swiftly changing tack in an attempt to prevent himself from experiencing further embarrassment in front of his younger colleague.

"Has Ella made any new friends recently? Ones who aren't in school? Say… erm… older people, late teens or beyond… Adults even?"

"What are you getting at?" asked Mrs Pollet, alarm showing on her face. "We've told you Ella's a good girl. She rarely goes out and when she does it's always with someone she knows… and someone we know too… and she always tells us where she's going. Ella isn't the sort to go off with strangers or anyone undesirable."

"I'm just asking, Ma'am," said Chalk, unabashed at the response, "so we can eliminate people from our enquiries. I don't mean to be rude or to cause offence, or to imply anything untoward."

There was silence for a moment, and then suddenly Benson leaned forward and spoke softly to Ella.

"Ella," he said gently. "In the classroom, when you disappeared, one of your friends thought she saw a small figure in your computer screen. I know you are finding it hard to remember but I'd like you to try really hard…

Does that stir any memory? Can you recall anything, a figure, or shape, in your computer screen?"

Chalk sat up abruptly and glowered at Benson threateningly, while Ella's parents seemed surprised at the line of questioning from Benson.

Ella just sat there still staring ahead. She made no reply. But Benson thought he saw a brief flicker in her eyes when he mentioned the figure in the screen, as if it brought some sort of momentary recognition. He was also aware of the tiniest of tears appearing in the corner of her eye. A tear which Ella hastily brushed away, with her hand, before anyone else could see it.

"Come on, Benson, we should be going," growled Chalk, standing up. He turned to Ella and her parents and in a voice filled with a mix of concern and charm said, "Thank you for your time. We'll be in touch as soon as we find anything. Goodbye."

Chalk rushed Benson out of the door. As they got into their car he snapped,

"What a ridiculous thing to ask, Benson. We've been through this before. I've told you that's all fanciful imagination. There's no mileage in it. You need to think before you open your mouth, Benson. Those parents will believe you are stupid… Well no… They will think the whole force is stupid if we are asking questions about little people in computers. You'll make the force a laughing stock, Benson, so in future you leave the questioning to me and you just stay in the background and only speak when I tell you!"

CHAPTER EIGHT

Three days later a Year 9 boy went missing from Hoblues. He was taking part in an after-school rugby match.

Zoe called all of her friends together in CAB, when the group met later that week.

"We missed that one, albeit he's not in our club but the timing is still about right."

She paused and looked around at the group of children gathered before her, then continued. "We have to be careful though. If we don't move quickly in trying to solve this mystery we'll find that whatever is behind it moves on to another school. Dan, have you got anything to report back on the radio transmitters?"

"I did find some," Daniel said. "But they were really expensive and I don't know how we'd get the money to buy any. Besides, I don't know enough about them to know if they're good value, or if they are up to the job we want them for. I really need to ask an adult."

"That could be tricky," Zoe replied. "We don't want any teachers to know and we certainly don't want any of our parents asking questions, but we do need to get a move on."

"I could ask one of the technicians," Daniel suggested. "Either one of the ICT ones or someone in the science department."

"Bit dodgy," reflected Zoe.

"You could say it was for a science project," Courtney offered.

"Then they might check with the science teachers," countered Zoe. "I know I seem like I'm being negative all the time but I am genuinely worried that we might get caught out and then our chance to find who is doing this will end and it will go on, because to be honest I don't think the police have got a clue judging by the way that Chalk bloke behaves."

"What if I asked my dad to help me?" Daniel began. "But if I told *him* it was for a science project. He wouldn't know any different, would he?"

"Probably not," agreed Zoe. "Try it, but do it tonight!"

Amy sat silently listening to the conversation. She was doing her best to think up some ideas, desperate to be able to do something to help. But her brain just wouldn't work right. Every time she tried to concentrate she got a pounding in her head. Not quite a headache but certainly bordering on one.

She shook her head as she attempted to clear it and get her concentration back, but the pounding continued. Suddenly she felt as if she was floating. The room began to move from side to side, gently at first, then more vigorously. It was shimmering now, like a heat haze, or a mirage that you might see in adventure films when someone is lost in a desert and they hallucinate and think they have found an oasis or are seeing a loved one about to rescue them. Amy could now hear her friend's voices getting more distant and distorted.

"What's happening to me?" she asked herself under her breath. "I don't feel well at all, and I rarely feel ill. I wonder if it's something I ate at lunchtime? I guess I'd better get off to the first aid room. I'll tell Mr Chatel I'm not well."

Amy prepared to stand so she could walk across to where the teachers were standing. As she did so she reached out a hand and touched Zoe on the arm.

"I'm just going to… "

Amy never got to finish the sentence. She just disappeared.

"Did you see that?" yelled Zoe. "Did you see what happened to Amy?"

"Look at the screen!" screamed Courtney. "Look at the screen!"

All eyes turned to the nearby computer and there in the corner of the screen a tiny figure could clearly be seen, only for a second, but it was definitely there. A small waving figure right down in the bottom corner of the screen, and it was wearing a Hoblues uniform.

CHAPTER NINE

Chalk and Benson were back in Chalk's office after a visit to Hoblues School, where they had interviewed the children and staff about the disappearance of Amy. Chalk was not best pleased by what he'd heard from the other CAB girls.

"I've told you before, Benson" growled Chalk. "Children have vivid imaginations which can be influenced by lots of things. This is exactly the same statement that one of those girls made when the last girl disappeared and that makes me doubly suspicious. Either they are trying to wind us up, or they are thinking about what was said last time and it's been playing on their minds to the extent that they've looked at the computer, seen a picture, and imagined it has happened this time as well."

"It might be true, Sir," said Benson.

"Nonsense," Chalk snorted. "Pull yourself together, Benson! You're supposed to be a detective, not a writer of fiction."

"But if it's happened twice, Sir, maybe we oughtn't to ignore it," argued Benson.

"It hasn't happened twice, Benson. It's just coincidence," snapped Chalk.

"I thought you didn't believe in coincidence, Sir," said Benson smugly.

"I don't," responded Chalk. "But I don't call this coincidence either. It's just a case of imagination and social hysteria brought on by the shock of having a friend vanish in front of your eyes."

"Psychologist now are you?" Benson muttered under his breath.

"What's that you say, Benson?" asked Chalk brusquely.

"Nothing, Sir," countered Benson. "Just wondering what a psychologist might make of it."

"We don't need psychologists, Benson," said Chalk gruffly. "We're detectives and that means we are going to solve this case by following clues, not by analysing some fantasy offered by hysterical teenagers. Now come on, we have to get statements from everyone else who was present and then go and talk to the missing girl's parents to see if they can offer any clues."

Benson looked across at Chalk and nodded his agreement, but in his mind he decided that he would follow up the story of a figure in the computer screen without his boss's knowledge. At least then he could safely put it to bed and look at alternatives if necessary. But in his heart he felt there was a lot more to this story than a young girl's imagination.

Like Ella before her, Amy closed her eyes and braced herself for the crash as she felt herself shrinking and then hurtling towards her computer screen, and like Ella she inwardly screamed and shouted that she didn't want to die.

Her shrunken tiny figure smashed straight through the screen and she was deposited on the other side shaken but unhurt.

Amy had one distinct advantage over Ella in as much as she was aware that people who disappeared did come back. She tried to get this small piece of knowledge to work in her favour by telling herself to stay calm and think. Quickly gathering her thoughts, she looked around the inside of the computer screen and she noticed that her friends were still visible on the other side.

"I'll give them a wave," she thought. "And hopefully they'll see me and get some idea of what is happening."

Amy began jumping up and down, at the same time waving her arms wildly and shouting. She could see Zoe and Courtney looking and pointing at the screen.

"I must look like some weird and demented goldfish," she thought, laughing silently to herself.

Just then the screen went blank and Amy was left alone in her unconventional and extraordinary prison.

She repeated her mantra about staying calm as she sat down to think. Whatever had brought her to this place would be coming for her soon. How soon she could only guess, but she couldn't believe it would wait for very long. And when it came… what then?

She gave a little shudder as she thought of what might await her. She was very scared and she could feel her heart pumping against her blouse as if it was trying to rip a hole in her and escape.

"Come on, Amy, pull yourself together. this is no time to give in and go to pieces," she thought. "What are you going to do?"

Amy breathed deeply and shook her head to clear it of the grisly images that were beginning to take over her mind. She thought back to Ella and the other children that had been taken and she suddenly knew that whatever was going to happen from now on, she wouldn't remember any of it.

If she was going to help her friends and the police to find out what had taken place whilst she was here, and so give them a chance to solve the mystery and to stop it happening again, then she had to find some way of keeping a record of events.

"What a pity that Dan couldn't have come up with his communication aids," Amy thought. "I could have been wired up now with everyone listening in and hearing all that's going to happen."

Aware of time, Amy hurriedly began to search in her pockets, desperately hoping to find something there that she could use, but all she came up with were some coins, a used tissue and her mobile phone. She was amused to find that these items had all shrunk with her.

"That's no good," she thought. "Courtney said I might not get a signal."

Amy stuffed the coins and the tissue back into her blazer pocket. She was about to do likewise with her phone when she had a thought. She held the phone in her hand for a second or two before switching it on.

"I'll try anyway," she said to herself. "You never know, Courtney could be wrong."

Amy's heartbeat quickened even more as she switched her phone on. She was pleased to see it light up in her now darkened prison, but seconds later her joy turned to disappointment as she discovered her friend had been right. There was a message clearly across the screen of her mobile proclaiming "NO SERVICE AVAILABLE. NO SIGNAL."

Amy muttered a rude word under her breath. She felt bitterly disappointed and she could feel her earlier fears returning. She switched off the phone and slipped it back into her pocket, but she kept a hand on it as her mind raced. Something was nagging in her brain, something to do with the phone. What was it?

Amy banged the palm of her free hand against her forehead.

"Come on! Come on! Think, Amy, think" she mused. "What is it? What are you trying to find? Think!"

After a few seconds which actually felt like years, Amy beat her brow again. She was struggling to find the thought that was hiding somewhere in her head. She let go her phone and it slipped down in her pocket, making a tinkling sound as it nestled against the coins.

Amy stood up. She decided she would have a walk around and explore the enclosed space that was now her prison cell.

"Who knows," she thought, "I might just find something I can use, or even a clue as to what will happen to me."

It was whilst she was poking around at what appeared to be a bunch of wires attached to the side of the screen wall that the elusive thought came back to her.

"Video camera."

The thought was crystal clear in her head. Her phone had a video camera.

"I don't need a signal for that," she thought excitedly. "I just need a fully charged battery and I charged my phone before I left home this morning. If I can find something to fix my phone to me, I can video what's happening."

Amy's fingers trembled as she took her phone from her blazer pocket again. She switched it on.

"I hope this works," she whispered to herself.

Amy pointed the face of the phone towards her, pressed the camera application and was immediately confronted with an image of herself on screen. She could barely contain her excitement.

"Brilliant," she said quietly. "Now all I need is to find something I can use to fix it on to myself and then to focus it so it can film and record but not be seen by whoever, or whatever, I am about to meet."

Amy looked at the bunch of wires near to where she was standing. They were just ordinary electrical wires sheathed in cable but because of Amy's shrunken size they looked enormous.

"Those are no good. They're much too big and heavy for me to do anything with," groaned Amy.

She was about to turn away and try to look elsewhere when her eyes focused on the ties that held the wires together. There was nothing special about them. They were just simple ties like the ones that people use every day to seal food or freezer bags, maybe a bit stronger as they were electrical ties, but they might prove to be useful none the less. Amy had an idea that she might be able to use them to hold her phone camera in place.

Amy reached up and grabbed at the nearest tie. Normally it would have been easy for her to undo it but as she was now so tiny the ties seemed huge and easily resisted her tiny fingers.

As she scrabbled at the ties Amy had no idea how long it would be before something happened to her or something came for her, but she knew she had to move fast if her plan was to be put into operation.

After what seemed an age, and with fingers now bleeding from the effort, Amy eventually managed to free one of the ties, but it was far too long.

Panicking, Amy looked around desperately for something to cut it with. There was nothing to hand.

Breathing heavily from her efforts at releasing the tie and frustrated that she couldn't proceed as there was nothing to cut it with, Amy sat on the floor and sobbed.

Inside her head a small voice brought her thoughts back to her plans.

"Come on, Amy, calm down," it said. "You have a great idea and if it works it can help to stop other people disappearing. OK, so you can't see anything to cut the tie with, so think and look around you. Think logically."

Amy breathed deeply again. She did look around and she did think logically and she saw the edge of the small metal cabinet that held the electrical cables.

"Bingo," she thought. "It's an edge… and it's metal… so that means it will cut."

Amy rose up and pulled the tie across to the metal casing. She began to rub the tie back and forth across the straight edge. She was really tired now from her efforts with freeing the tie and with hauling it across to the casing, and her exertions in rubbing it back and forth had taken their toll on her energy levels and on her now diminutive frame. Amy wanted to rest. She wanted to sleep. But she knew that if she did all would be lost and she would never be able to put her plan into action.

"One last effort," she urged herself.

Amy summoned up her last ounces of strength and energy. She rubbed hard and long and eventually she felt the harsh stiff binding begin to lose its tension. A few more rubs and it gave way completely.

Amy sat down again. Her breathing was harsh and rasping.

"No time to rest," she chided. "Finish the job."

She leaned against the metal wall behind her and closed her eyes as she fought to get her breathing under some sort of control.

Suddenly she was aware of a noise some distance away and to her left… footsteps… and they were coming towards her.

Amy sat bolt upright. Her blood stained fingers fumbled desperately for her phone. She grasped it in her shaking hands and switched on the video camera. Hands trembling, she hooked one end of the tie through the small aperture in the top of her phone, then undoing the top two buttons of her blouse she slipped the phone under her blouse so that the camera lens was peeping out through the gap left after fastening the top button. Amy then secured the other end of the tie to the buttonhole beneath the button so that the camera was filming and recording but couldn't be easily seen.

She had only just managed to secure the phone when a door opened at the side of her prison. She was scared now. Heart beating a rapid tattoo, Amy glanced towards the light that flooded into the prison cell. She was really scared. Scared of what was going to happen to her and scared of what might happen if her attempts to video events came to light and her phone camera was discovered.

As Amy stared at the door she saw what appeared to be a well-dressed man. He was wearing a dark suit, a white shirt and black tie. He looked a bit like a butler that Amy had once seen in a television drama. He came over to where Amy was sitting.

"You will come with me," he ordered.

Amy stood up. The man towered over her.

"Who are you? And why am I here?" said Amy defiantly, her cracked voice betraying her inner fear.

"You will come with me," ordered the man again, pointing towards the door.

"Where are you taking me?" yelled Amy, now crying.

"You will come with me," repeated the man, his voice without emotion.

"What if I won't go?" said Amy, stubbornly refusing to move.

"You will come with me." The reply was the same.

"Is that all you can say?" asked Amy, now curious, and annoyed, about the constant repetition.

"You will come with me," repeated the man for the fifth time.

Amy decided she was not going to get any other answer and she didn't know how long he would go on repeating this phrase before either he or someone else took further action. She didn't want to make him angry or to antagonise anyone who might be waiting for her, so she made a forward move. The man looked at her and stepped back.

"You will come with me," he said flatly and then turned on his heel and walked away. Amy cautiously followed him through the door.

When she got outside of her prison Amy caught up with the man and suddenly realised that she was now as tall as he was.

"Either he's shrunk or I've returned to my normal size," she said to no one in particular. Then, more directly, she asked the man, "Which one is it?"

"You will come with me" was the monotonous reply.

Amy followed the man along a lengthy corridor and eventually they emerged through another door into an open area that had the appearance of a large warehouse.

There were a number of storage racks on which loads of boxes stood. The racks stretched for a long way into the distance and were set alongside each other to produce aisles and walkways between each rack.

The light was too dim for Amy to see the boxes in any great detail but at the far end of the warehouse she could see light. There was some movement there too. She couldn't quite see what it was but something was certainly moving.

Amy screwed up her eyes and stared ahead towards the movement. As they got closer she thought she could see a tall white shape. She was alongside the man in the dark suit and about to ask him what it was when he reached out his hand and touched the back of her neck. Then she passed out.

CHAPTER TEN

Amy sat stone faced and stared straight ahead as DCI Chalk began his questioning. Benson sat alongside him as he spoke.

"So, er… Amy, isn't it?" Chalk began hesitantly. "Can you tell us what happened to you?"

Benson sighed inwardly and raising his eyebrows he shook his head slowly from side to side. There were times when he despaired of his superior officer and this was one of those times.

"This girl has just come back from whatever ordeal she has been through and Chalk expects her to remember everything about it when none of the others have been able to, and he even has trouble remembering her name," thought Benson. "Chalk really does need to wise up on this case. Whatever is happening here it is something out of the ordinary but all he does is ask the same inflexible questions. He can be a real pain with his rigid beliefs and in my view his fixed ideas are stopping us progressing in our bid to solve the case."

Amy did not move. She continued to stare at the wall opposite her. Chalk's eyes never left her face as his mouth pursed into a look of disapproval.

"Amy love.", It was Amy's mum who broke the silence that had descended on the room like a rolling fog. "Please try to answer the detective's questions and if you can remember then say so," she encouraged gently.

Benson leapt to Amy's defence. "It's all right, Amy," he said soothingly. "It's quite normal for children who have been through this to be unable to remember."

Benson was aware that Chalk was glaring at him. He could almost see the steam coming out of Chalk's ears as he leaned forward and addressed the girl again.

"Come on, Amy," Chalk pleaded urgently, "Try harder. Come on. Anything… anything at all that might help us."

Amy just sat staring.

"Oh for goodness sake, girl," Chalk exploded impatiently. "It's only just happened. You've only been back ten minutes, surely you can't have forgotten already. Something must have stuck in your head!"

It was Benson's turn to glare at Chalk. He was about to apologise on behalf of his colleague when Amy's mum jumped in to her rescue.

"Yes, she has only been back for ten minutes," she snapped. "And might I remind you she's been missing for a whole week and no one knows what has happened to her in that time. She is obviously in shock so I don't think you speaking to her like that is going to make her feel any better or free up her memory, do you?"

The Detective Inspector recoiled in the face of Mrs Tallon's verbal onslaught.

"Sorry, Ma'am," he apologised. "It's just that we can never seem to get any information from anyone and I thought that as it might still be fresh in your daughter's mind she might remember something. I didn't mean to shout. I just got frustrated and a bit carried away in my quest for information and clues about what is happening."

With that Chalk rose from his chair. "Come on, Benson. We're going. There's nothing for us here," he muttered lamely.

Chalk and Benson left the house and walked to their car.

"Why don't they remember, Benson?" Chalk asked despairingly.

"Don't know, Sir," replied Benson. "Perhaps whoever or whatever is taking them does something to their memory. Maybe it hypnotises them or gives them something to make them forget."

Chalk's face lit up at Benson's words.

"Drugs," he said animatedly as he returned to his favourite theory. "I told you it was drugs, Benson. They can do that to your memory."

"Yes, they can," Benson agreed. "But she's only been away for a week. You heard what that Medical Consultant said. You know the one I'm talking about, the parent of Ella Pollet who also disappeared. The amount of drugs she'd have to take in a week to make her memory that bad would be enough to kill her."

"Maybe not," Chalk responded brightly. "Not if it was one special drug that could wipe out memory immediately. Check it out, Benson. Consultants or doctors don't know everything. I'm sure there must be some drug that fits the bill."

"Of course, it could be the shock of everything that's happened to them that causes their memory to blank out," mused Benson. "Like a psychological block... I've heard of that happening to soldiers and to people who have been in really bad accidents or when they have lost someone near and dear."

"I've told you before, Benson," barked Chalk savagely. "We don't deal in psychology. We deal in fact. Now when we get back you go and check out that drug for me, and I don't want to hear any more about psychology."

After Chalk and Benson had left Amy's home Mrs Tallon sat next to her daughter and put a comforting arm around her.

"Whatever has happened to you, Amy, you know I'll stand by you. You'll always be my baby and I'll try my best to help and support you through this."

"Leave me alone, you sad, stupid moron," screamed Amy. "I don't want your help or your support and I don't want you interfering in my life. I'll deal with this my way. Now I'm going to my room and I'll probably be there for the rest of the day, so don't even bother to come up and try to sneak in to see if I'm all right because I'm barricading the door."

She got up and rushed upstairs, slamming the lounge door. Behind her she could hear the sound of her mother sobbing loudly.

In her room Amy began to throw her things about. She felt very angry but didn't know why. She stomped around the room hurling anything that came to hand. Mrs Tallon sat in the lounge crying as she listened to her daughter banging and crashing about in the room above her head.

"Oh Amy, what's happened to you?" she wept. "Where's my beautiful, caring baby gone?"

In the bedroom above Amy was now in full swing. Clothes, make-up, ornaments, CDs, DVDs, it didn't matter what it was, if it was in the way it was hurled feverishly and angrily across the room. Amy wasn't in a mood for thinking so she was unable to distinguish between the breakable and the unbreakable, or the costly and the cheap. It wasn't long before she ran out of handily available things to throw.

With anger still burning inside her, Amy felt in her pockets and then in her blouse, where she located her mobile phone. Without any thought she grasped the phone and flung it on to her bed. Then she walked towards her wardrobe to start on her shoes and the rest of her clothes.

Seconds later Amy froze in her tracks as a voice she vaguely knew, from somewhere within her subconscious, began speaking. Amy felt herself tremble and shake. She felt a cold hand clutch at her heart and panic spread its clammy, creeping fingers around her abdomen.

"That voice!" she thought. "Why is it making me feel like this, so terrified and filled with fear?"

In the short time since her return she'd been aware of a continuous anger inside of her, not only anger but a desire to hurt people and to be destructive. She had no idea why she felt like this. In the absence of memory, she'd assumed that was how she'd always been but now, hearing that voice, in addition to the terror it brought her, she was strangely conscious of something new happening inside her head.

There was a thought nagging in her brain. It wasn't a great awakening, just a slight discomfort. A bit like when you hear a song on the radio and you know you should know the title and the singer because it's in your iPod collection and you've listened to it a thousand times. But you can't for the life of you remember and the more you try to think the further away the answer recedes, until your brain hurts and you end up frustrated and furious and eventually your brain gives up the ghost and you return to who you are. That's when the answer springs back into your head as if to mock all of your previous efforts to remember. Either that or the radio DJ tells you who and what it is and you give yourself a mental kick in the pants for being so lame brained.

Amy was experiencing that feeling of discomfort right now. The voice coming from her phone was soft, gentle and soothing, yet there was something sinister about it and her mind and body were reacting to it as if it was a huge threat and something to be scared of, and in that tiny corner of her brain the nagging thought persisted. Amy knew that voice, but from where? She had the feeling that she'd met the owner of the voice and somehow the experience had changed her.

Amy sat down on the bed next to her phone. She listened intently as the voice informed her that it was about to take a part of her away. She leaned forward. The sound quality on the phone wasn't good at this point as the background noise of some kind of electrical equipment being started up took over from the voice which, although still speaking, had faded rapidly. Amy could still hear it if she put her ear right to the phone. She resisted the urge to recoil from the frightening sound emanating from the instrument and forced herself to listen to the spoken words.

"My travelling companions and I are about to transport into my collection the part of you that I believe you humans call your personality, although I think that some people prefer to call it your spirit or your soul.

"It will not hurt you if you stay still, but struggling will cause my companions to take action by holding you down. You should know that they are strong, and also as they do not feel pain themselves they will not recognise whether they are hurting you or not, so struggling may bring you even more pain.

"During the transportation process please do not try to withhold or block your thoughts as this will cause emergency mind-clearing waves to activate. If this occurs you will experience severe head pain and your mind may be totally wiped, leaving you without any thought and deprived of the capacity for future thought.

"If the transportation is successful you will need time to recover, so you will remain here for one of your Earth weeks. You will then be transported to a place near to your home. You will be as you are now physically, but your emotional and mental state will have undergone some changes as you will only retain negative personality traits, which everyone who undergoes this process has, regardless of the image that they choose to show to the world.

"Furthermore, you will remember nothing about what you have undergone whilst here. You will still retain your previous memories of who you are, who are your parents and friends, and you will also be able to remember most things about your life but you will only remember these from a negative perspective. It may also take some time before your memory is fully functioning again, but even when it is there will be no memory of you being here.

"Do not be afraid, my child. I have no intention of killing you or deliberately hurting you, so I suggest you lie back and relax while my companions perform their tasks."

The voice was then lost to screaming and the throbbing sound of machinery and electrical impulses.

Amy gave an involuntary shudder.

"Why is this person on my phone?" she asked herself. "And why does it scare me so much?"

She picked up her phone and yelled into it.

"STOP IT! Get off my phone!… Who are you?… How did you get my number?"

The screaming continued. Amy fumbled for the button to cut off the call. She found it and pressed hard on it. The throbbing and screaming didn't stop.

Amy began to cry. She looked closely at her phone to see what was wrong. It was then that she noticed it was on video replay.

"It must have clicked on to that when I threw my phone on to my bed," she thought. "But what was that I was listening to and where did I get it? I can't remember recording it, but then I can't remember too much at the moment. Perhaps it was part of a film or TV show I've recorded for someone."

Amy peered at the small screen on her phone. All that was visible was a large ceiling light. The kind you see in hospital operating theatres. She watched for a while but the scene didn't change and the infernal noise, that was now beginning to make her angry again, continued unabated.

Amy quickly thumbed through the options and apps on her phone and settled on rewind. She pressed the screen, let a few minutes go by, and then pressed the application that allowed her to replay.

Amy's heart, which had been busy beating out a loud and rapid drumbeat since she'd first heard the voice, now performed a double somersault and almost burst out of her chest as she was confronted by the face that was now visible on the screen. It wasn't just any old face. It wasn't even a normal face. The face staring at her from the small screen was completely devoid of colour.

It looked like a human face, but it was pure white as if painted in emulsion, and the rims of the eyes, the sockets and the eyes themselves were black as soot, as were the lips and mouth. The face had no teeth as far as Amy could tell, and a closer inspection showed her that the eyes were without pupils or irises. They appeared to be two large holes in the head, yet they had depth and movement and when the owner of the face blinked, which wasn't that often, Amy caught the merest flash of white where the pupils should be, like a camera lens flashing.

It was a frightening and alarming face and Amy wondered why it was on the video camera on her mobile phone. She watched for a while but there was no sound other than the odd clink and whirring noise in the background.

Suddenly the owner of the face backed away. Behind him in the background Amy could see a wall with racks and shelves on which several boxes, or what looked like boxes, were stacked. As she peered intently at the screen Amy caught a glimpse of a figure. It was a man, and he was dressed in a dark suit with a white shirt and black tie. Behind him stood another man dressed exactly the same.

Amy felt a slight stirring in her brain. What was it? What was she trying to remember? She tried hard to think, but as before nothing came.

Her eyes darted back to the screen. The racks and the men were moving. Amy stared at the image before her. She was puzzled. They were moving all right… but upwards.

"How is that possible? What's happening," Amy asked herself quietly

Then the men and the racks settled but this time they were a little higher up on the screen, and the face had disappeared. Amy was quickly able to figure out that their previous movement had been caused by the camera angle being changed. From this deduction she guessed that whoever was holding the camera had shifted their position so that, whether sitting or standing, they were now tilting backwards.

The face came back into view, but this time it was further away and Amy was now able to see the body too. The person, whoever he was, was tall and slim, much taller than the men in dark suits. He, in direct contrast, was dressed from head to foot in a white suit with a black shirt and a white tie. The face had no hair, it was completely bald. As Amy watched a bony hand moved out from the body, took hold of something from off screen and placed it on his head. It was a white top hat. Amy laughed. Far from being sinister the figure now looked as if it had come straight out of an old Hollywood musical, like the ones she used to watch with her grandma, when she was younger.

Amy was surprised that she remembered that fact, but that was it, she had no other memories at present. Looking back at the screen she smiled once more as she observed that the figure had taken on the appearance of a grotesque cartoon character, and she felt the tension inside her lessen with her amusement.

The picture moved again, and now she was looking at the ceiling light again and the face began to speak in its soft, gentle tones.

"Relax, my child," it said. "My travelling companions and I are about to transport into my collection the part of you that I believe you humans call your personality, although I think that some people prefer to call it your spirit or your soul… "

Amy switched off her phone. She had been here before and didn't like it. She racked her brains to think of why this was on her phone. She couldn't remember ever seeing these people before, but they were there on her phone and it didn't look to her as if they were part of a film or TV drama that had been recorded at a cinema or in someone's front room, as she could see no intruding images from other people sitting in the cinema, and there were no shapes or deteriorations in the shades of colour in the picture to suggest it was recorded from a TV screen. Additionally the sound quality was infinitely better than you could expect if it had been taken from either of these two media.

"So that must mean that, either someone took my phone and made the whole film up as a practical joke, or that I recorded it myself," Amy muttered. "And I can't believe anyone I know would be able to come up with anything that realistic and chilling if they were doing it for a joke, especially as it would cost them for costumes and scenery. So that leaves me! I must have done it. But when and why?"

Amy tried to think again.

"Drat my memory," she cursed out loud. "Why can't I remember?"

Amy lay back on her bed. Her phone lay alongside her. She picked it up and held it in her hand, turning it over several times as she wrestled with her memory block.

"I must have recorded it," she repeated. "But I can't for the life of me think when. But I do know that whoever that voice belongs to I must have heard it before because when it came on my phone just now it scared the life out of me."

Amy paused for more reflection, then shivered as a thought hit her. "Which means that whenever or for whatever reason I recorded it, I sure didn't do it for fun or pleasure. So it might have something to do with what mum and those policemen keep referring to as my disappearance. Now I can't remember disappearing but they tell me I did and that I was away for a whole week!"

Amy sat up abruptly and slapped her open palm against her forehead.

"Come on, think, girl… think… what's the connection?"

She sighed as her brain refused to come up with an answer. Amy punched the headboard in frustration, yelling out in pain as she did so. She rubbed her hand and then suddenly all thought of her pain was gone as something clicked inside her head.

"A week! I was missing for a week!" she said. "That voice… in the video. It said you will remain here for a week. There's the link. I must have somehow managed to record that video whilst I was away and if so then it could hold important clues about where I've been and what's happened to my memory."

Amy cheered up a bit at this thought, even though she knew deep inside she was still scared and confused, and would remain so until she got to the truth about what had happened to her.

"The voice said it was going to take my personality… my soul," she said. "It also said it was going to wipe out my memory. I guess that's why I'm so angry and struggling to remember. My soul has been snatched from me and I wasn't supposed to know how or why. But I've got that recording and at least I can understand what has happened, if not why. And I can still remember things about my life before I disappeared, but I can't remember much happiness, just as that creature said I would. So I guess that confirms my theory that what's on that tape is what happened to me."

Amy took a deep breath and stood up. She went over to her mirror where she stared at her reflection. Her face showed signs of tension and tiredness. She flexed her mouth and her lips and pulled a few faces, trying to relieve some of the rigidity and tautness that was clearly visible around her eyes and mouth. Then she spoke to her mirror image.

"Well, Mr Soul Snatcher," she said defiantly. "You are going to get a surprise. For once someone knows about you and your evil deeds, and all I need to do now is to show this recording to someone who can track you down and stop you!"

Amy began to feel excited. She now had hope and that hope helped to make her anger and frustration start to subside.

"Right," she said determinedly, "I need to find someone I can trust and let them see this video."

"Are you all right, Amy love?" Her mother's voice rang out from outside her bedroom. It was accompanied by a loud knock on the bedroom door. "Can I come in?"

"I can't let mum see this video," Amy thought. "She wouldn't understand. She'd probably freak out, and in any case she'd only tell me I'm fantasising and then ignore it, or worse still take it straight to the police."

"Yes, I'm all right," Amy shouted to her mum. "And you can come in, but give me a minute first."

Amy hurriedly shoved her phone into one of her bedside drawers.

"You can come in now, Mum," she yelled.

Mrs Tallon entered the room. She stopped in her tracks as she saw the mess created by Amy throwing everything around in her rage. Mrs Tallon felt the anger rise inside her as she surveyed the vista of scattered clothes and pillows, the broken picture frames and DVD and CD cases, and the mixture of perfume, mascara and make-up remover that was steadily dripping from the surface of the dressing table and on to the bedroom carpet.

She was about to yell at her daughter that this was disgraceful and unacceptable and tell her to clean it up at once, and to tell her that she was grounded for a week. But the thought that her only child had been missing and could easily have not returned, or even been killed, suddenly shot into her head. Mrs Tallon's angry words sank back inside her and instead she rushed over to the bed where Amy sat. She reached out, put her arms around Amy and hugged her tightly.

"Oh Amy… Amy… my precious," she cried. "I'm so glad you're back. I've been so scared and worried. Don't you bother about this mess, I'll help you clean it up. Then we'll get a takeaway, eh? Are you all right my love?"

"Yes, Mum," said Amy, "I'm fine."

"I heard you talking to someone as I came up the stairs. Have you been on the phone?" mum asked.

"No," replied Amy sharply. "I was just talking to myself… you know, thinking out loud."

"You should call some of your friends, dear. It might help you feel better and settle in again," Mrs Tallon ventured. "By the way, have you still got your mobile? I haven't seen it while you've been away so I assumed you'd taken it with you. Why didn't you use it to phone me?"

"Stop fussing, Mum," hissed Amy. "I've still got my phone. It's around somewhere and I didn't phone you because I don't remember where I was or what I've done, so for all I know I might not have been in a position to phone anyone. For goodness' sake I've only been back a few hours and you're already on to me asking why I didn't phone and have I got my phone and why don't I call my friends. Leave me alone. I'll clear this mess up by myself… just go… I'll come down later."

"All right, dear, if that's how you feel. I'll see you later," said Mrs Tallon, getting up from the bed and heading towards the door. She paused as she reached it and with one hand on the handle turned to Amy.

"Can I get you anything?" she asked. "Something to eat or drink, some juice maybe?"

"MUM… JUST GO!" yelled Amy.

Mrs Tallon gave a sigh and shaking her head slowly she opened the door and went downstairs. Amy got up from the bed and closed the door that her mum had left open.

"Oh no you don't!" she muttered. "I know you, leaving the door open so you can hear if I use my phone."

Amy returned to her bed. The cleaning up could wait. She needed to think first about who she could give the video to. The obvious person would be DI Chalk, but Amy didn't like him.

"He's too grumpy and fixed in his ways," she thought. "I bet if I gave it to him he'd say I'd made it all up just to cover up what really happened. I could give it to his assistant, he's nice, but then he'd only give it to Chalk."

Amy went through a mental list of people. Teachers? No, they'd have to hand it to the police... Dad? No way! From what I can remember of my past he hardly bothers to see me anyway, and he hasn't been around or called to see if I'm all right since I've been back. In the end Amy decided she'd give it to someone in CAB, perhaps either Zoe or Simran.

Because of the negative views that were now a part of her thought processes, she was unsure if she could trust them, or even if she wanted to. She wasn't even sure if they were still her friends, but she had to find someone to help her and when needs must... Amy made a decision to take the video into the next CAB meeting.

"They'll know what to do with it," she thought.

CHAPTER ELEVEN

"See, I told you as much, didn't I?," Chalk beamed triumphantly. "There's quite a list here. Well done, Benson. Now we're getting somewhere."

He was reading through the list of drugs, with short-term memory loss identified as a side effect, that Benson had prepared for him.

"Look," said Chalk excitedly, as he jabbed a finger on to different areas of the paper in front of him. "Benzodiazepenes. They can calm you down, and what about this one, Ambien, that one is for helping you to sleep."

"How do you know all of this?" asked Benson, impressed by his colleague's apparent medical knowledge.

"My mother was prescribed both when I was younger," answered Chalk.

"But you can't seriously be thinking that those children who disappeared would have all been prescribed those sort of drugs?" queried Benson.

"Their mothers could have them on prescription," Chalk said emphatically. "And the kids could have taken some to their parties or wherever it was they went."

"You've seen their mothers. Do you honestly believe that any, let alone all of them, would be taking those? Or if they were, wouldn't have noticed if some had gone missing?" Benson asked, no longer impressed by his boss, just annoyed at his lack of understanding and vision.

Chalk didn't answer, so Benson continued his defence. "You've met the children too, and heard what they were like from parents and teachers. Every child who has gone missing was well balanced, well adjusted, considerate and friendly. And all were achieving well in school. Does that sound like a group of people that would have anything to do with drugs?" he demanded.

Chalk remained silent as his finger moved down the page and stopped abruptly alongside one of the names written there. Then he turned to Benson with a smirk on his face.

"What about this one then, eh, Benson,?" he shrieked. "Even you can't find fault with this, and they wouldn't have to rely on their parents for it either."

"What's that then, Sir?" asked Benson indifferently.

"Ecstasy!" said Chalk loudly. "Ecstasy, Benson. They wouldn't have to take that with them. They can get it there. Right, lad, that's our lead, let's get on to the drugs squad and get them to follow it up."

Chalk walked off whistling happily. Benson trudged behind him, gloom written all over his face.

Two days later at the CAB group Amy sidled up to Zoe and Simran. She had been back in school on both days since her return and to her dismay had found that although her longer-term memory was still functioning reasonably well, it wasn't quite good enough in remembering who, if anyone, she was close to in school.

Not that she felt particularly close to anyone in her current state. She wanted to be left alone. But of course everyone wanted to know where she'd been and they'd crowded around her asking endless questions until she lost her temper and told them all where to go.

Inside Amy felt a strange mix of anger, anxiety and hate. This was coupled with a desire to hurt and be horrible to anyone who crossed her path, especially anyone who looked as if they were happy and having fun. For Amy the two days passed very slowly. She found herself being snappy and unpleasant to everyone, including teachers, which landed her with the first detention she'd ever had.

In CAB Amy felt strange. This was where she'd disappeared from, and everyone had told her that she was sucked into the computer. But she couldn't remember, and to be honest she didn't believe them, and had told them all as much.

Now she could see everyone enjoying themselves and working on their own projects. She felt alone and left out and this wasn't helped by the fact that the others, whilst not exactly ignoring her, were none the less giving her a wide berth following her earlier angry outbursts and tantrums.

Zoe and Simran were showing each other what they'd produced on their computer screens. They were laughing and joking with each other. The laughter stopped at Amy's approach and they looked at her warily as she edged along the desk beside them.

"Hi, Amy," said Zoe hesitantly. "Good to have you back."

"Yeah... How are you?" Simran asked warily.

"Could be better, I suppose," replied Amy edgily.

They continued to make small talk for a while but it was a stilted and uneasy conversation. Zoe and Simran were clearly ill at ease with Amy in her present state.

Amy gathered her thoughts and fought to rid herself of the negativity inside her. She needed these two to see her video and to do whatever was necessary to ensure it was followed up properly so that the Soul Snatcher could be stopped.

Amy drew a deep breath.

"Listen, you guys," she said. "I know I'm not the same as I used to be. I know I'm angry and horrible now and I think that's because of something that happened to me when I was away, but I really need you guys to help me get back to how I was."

Simran looked up and Amy could see suspicion and apprehension in her eyes.

"And how do we do that?" Simran asked warily.

"I've got something I want to show you," said Amy. "I think it might explain better than I can."

She took out her phone and switched it on to video play.

"Take a look at this," she said, thrusting the phone towards Zoe and Simran.

Just then Daniel wandered across and peered over Zoe's shoulder. The three of them watched open mouthed as the video played out the scene recorded by Amy.

"Hey, that's wicked," laughed Daniel. "That guy in the white suit. He's something else. Is he for real? What's with the fancy dress and the face paint? That must have been some party you went to, Amy. Who is that guy? And when are we gonna meet him? You should put that on You Tube. It will get some massive hits."

Amy closed her eyes.

"I knew it," she thought. "They're not going to believe me."

"Dan!… SHUT UP!" snapped Zoe. She turned to Amy. "Is this for real?" she asked.

Amy nodded.

"You recorded this whilst you were away?" Simran was the next to respond.

Again Amy nodded.

"So what?" asked Daniel. "It's just some guy dressing up and pretending he's a cool villain."

"Oh Daniel, are you really that dim?" asked Simran. "This isn't pretend."

"No," echoed Zoe, "you're missing the point, Daniel. This isn't about what the guy looks like, or about entertaining people on You Tube. This is really serious. Whoever that guy is, he's taking people's personalities and minds away. That's why Amy and Ella have changed. That's why they have both become so crabby and are acting differently in a kind of horrible way."

Zoe looked back at Amy. "But if that… that… that thing. Whatever he is… "

"I call him the Soul Snatcher," Amy interrupted.

"Whatever," said Zoe. "The Soul Snatcher or whoever. If he's taking people's minds away and making them different, why is he doing it? And what's he getting out of it?"

"So you've been brainwashed by that guy in the white suit and that's why you're like this now?" said Daniel to Amy, who nodded again.

"I think we should show this to someone," said Simran.

"Like who?" asked Zoe, with a trace of irritation in her voice.

"Mr Nilson and Mr Chatel" Simran replied.

"Yeah, and what are they gonna do with it?" queried Zoe sarcastically. "Just give it back to us and let us track him down?"

"Suppose not," mumbled Simran. "But have you got any better ideas?"

"Not yet," said Zoe. "But I'm working on it."

"What's that you've got there, Zoe?"

The voice of Mr Nilson made all four jump. He was standing right behind them. No one had heard him approach. They had all been so engrossed in discussing the video.

"I hope it's not your mobile. You know the rules about mobile phones being used in school so put it away please."

"It's mine, Sir," said Amy and reached out to take it from Zoe. "I'll put it in my bag. Sorry, Sir."

She took the phone and went to put it into her bag, but in doing so her finger accidentally pressed on play. Instantly the voice of the Soul Snatcher came loud and clear from the direction of Amy's bag, recounting again what he intended to do to Amy.

"Blast," muttered Zoe. She saw Amy and Simran wince and turned slightly to face them so she could mouth a warning for them not to say anything.

"What *is* that, Amy?" asked Mr Nilson. "It sounds pretty frightening. Where did you get it?"

Amy was about to tell Mr Nilson that it was a TV drama she had recorded to show the others when Daniel piped up.

"You should see it, Mr Nilson. It's really wicked. It's some guy in fancy dress telling Amy that he's going to take away her mind. It's awesome."

Zoe slumped forward in her seat, her head in her hands.

"Well done, Dan, you idiot," she whispered through clenched teeth. "Now he's gonna take it to the police."

"Let me see it, Amy, please," said Mr Nilson, holding out his hand for the phone.

Amy handed it over and the four of them sat silently as Mr Nilson replayed the video.

"Is this genuine?" he asked when it was finished.

Simran nodded. "Amy switched on her video camera whilst she was away and that's what was on it when she came back home," she said.

"Who else has seen this?" Mr Nilson asked Amy.

"Only us four," she replied.

"This could be a vital clue as to what happened, not only to you, Amy, but to all of the other children who have gone missing," Mr Nilson said. "I'll need to take it to Mrs Stewber and she'll have to hand it to the police, but just to make sure it doesn't go astray I'm going to make a spare copy on the computer and keep it in my personal documents."

"Thanks a bunch, Dan, you big mouth," growled Zoe as Mr Nilson went off with Amy's phone. "It's out of our hands now and soon it will be with that Inspector Clown or whatever his name is… What is his name? Chalk, yeah, that's him, and heaven knows what he'll do with it. Oh Danny, why did you have to open your mouth like that. We could have just pretended it was a play or something."

"Sorry," said Daniel, shamefaced and hanging his head. "I didn't think. I was really excited by it all and Mr Nilson is all right, I guess I just got carried away."

As this conversation was taking place the video was already on its way to DI Chalk.

"Very clever," said Chalk, appreciatively. "Very clever indeed, Benson. These children should become film makers when they leave school. They have great imagination and invention, not to mention a penchant for the theatrical, as expressed in the costume and make-up."

"You think it's a fake?" asked Benson incredulously.

"Of course it's a fake, Benson," chortled Chalk. "A good fake, but a fake none the less. Well put together. You notice they've avoided the age-old stereotype about little green men or monsters, but they've still tried to make it into a sci-fi or horror film."

"But it looks genuine, Sir," said Benson. "And it fits the pattern and nature of the disappearances and what the children are like when they return. I think we should investigate it further before we rule it out."

"Of course it fits the pattern, Benson," said Chalk glibly. "That's what it's designed for. This, Benson, is a very well put together documentation of what happens to the children who go missing... And it's made to fool us... to steer us away from finding out what is really happening... to stop us finding their parties and their drugs."

"But there's no way the children could have concocted that, Sir," argued Benson, who was getting agitated with his boss. "Who is the guy in white? *He's* an adult. And who are the men in dark suits? And where would they get access to an operating theatre, for goodness' sake?"

"They must have got their parents involved," said Chalk. "And as for the operating theatre, Benson, remember that girl? What was her name? Ellie, Ellen... ah, Ella .. that's her. Wasn't her dad a doctor or a consultant or something? He could easily have arranged to borrow an operating theatre out of hours, and done some filming. He wouldn't need it for long. That video was only about 15 minutes in total."

Benson shook his head in disbelief. Chalk continued undeterred.

"Maybe the parents are behind these disappearances... perhaps hoping to sue the schools for not looking after their children. Compensation and damages claims pay out quite a bit of money these days, Benson... Hmm now that is a thought. Yes… Hmm, I think we'll go back and talk to those parents again, Benson. I'm sure they're hiding something."

Benson looked up to the heavens in despair as Chalk strode from the office, hurriedly beckoning his assistant to follow.

CHAPTER TWELVE

Benson had had enough of Chalk. Everything the man had seen relating to possible areas of investigation, and every potential clue which had begged further scrutiny, Chalk had dismissed as irrelevant. He had a closed mind. He didn't want to look elsewhere. Chalk was convinced that his theories about drugs and cults and parties had been right, and as each one had been investigated and resulted in a dead end, so Chalk saw this as a conspiracy to stop him finding what he believed to be the truth.

Even when the drugs squad had recently told Chalk that his latest theory didn't hold water, instead of accepting what they said, which was based on their years of experience, he'd said he would prove them wrong, since when he'd spent a lot of time surfing the web in a bid to do just that.

Then there was his theory about parents suing schools, and borrowing operating theatres. Chalk had made a right fool of himself when he'd put that to the parents, especially to the Medical Consultant, who had been so angry he'd threatened to go to the Chief Constable. Chalk had averted this by apologising, but he still clung on to his theory in the privacy of his office.

Benson was concerned that all this sidetracking was diverting investigation away from the truth. He worried that whoever, or whatever, was responsible for the disappearance and subsequent personality change and memory loss of these children would soon move on, or that the incidences would increase significantly and many other children would be similarly harmed. He didn't believe that these events would continue indefinitely. He was convinced that whatever was happening was time limited. Hence it was essential that they solved this case as quickly as possible.

Benson had two choices now as he saw it. Either he could confront Chalk, and tell him what he thought about the way he was conducting the case, or he could go to the Superintendent and tell him how he felt and what he believed should be done.

"Not good either way," Benson said to himself. "If I confront Chalk, he won't change his mind. He's not that sort of person. So, he'll probably go to the Super and have me removed from the case. And if I go straight to the Super, the Super might think I'm getting above myself and so take no notice of what I say, but tell Chalk and then remove me from the case anyway."

Benson pondered his dilemma. There was a third alternative. Just get on with it and let Chalk have his own way.

"I can't do that," thought Benson. "He'll never solve it, and then I would have any further disappearances on my conscience, knowing I could have at least said something and maybe changed the course of the enquiry."

Benson poured himself a cup of coffee and pondered his dilemma.

Half an hour later Benson was knocking on the Superintendent's office door.

"Come," said a loud voice.

Benson went in and closed the door behind him.

He emerged an hour later, red in the face, but with a feeling of relief and satisfaction. There was a new spring in his step too, and a new belief in himself.

The Superintendent had listened to his concerns, stared at him intently as he explained his own theories and thoughts of what he believed the clues meant. The Super had rubbed his hand across his chin as he reflected on what had been said, then left the room for a while, and when he returned said,

"Right, DI Chalk is off the case, at least temporarily. Don't worry, I'll let him down gently. I'm putting you in charge, Benson. We need to solve this case quickly. The media are getting restless and really going to town on this, and the Local Authority and Members of Parliament are getting worried about the public being scared by what's happening. They think parents will start to keep their children away from school if this continues, and they're also concerned about the public losing faith in the police and the government.

"I'll assign you a couple of DCs, and if there's anything else you need, just ask. Follow up your clues. I know they sound far fetched, but we're desperate and who knows? Strange things are happening so maybe we need to investigate strange theories, and who's to say? Perhaps they're right."

"Thank you, Sir, I won't let you down," said Benson, resisting the urge to break into a grin and punch the air.

He turned to leave the office.

"Oh, one thing, Benson," said the Superintendent.

Benson paused, hand on the door handle. "Yes, Sir?" he queried.

"I'll take care of all the press conferences and deal with the media circus, but I'll expect you to keep me up to date with what you're doing so we don't get caught with our pants down."

"Yes, Sir, of course," said Benson. He opened the door and walked back to his office.

Benson was studying the mobile phone video again when Chalk walked in.

"Judas," snarled Chalk, glaring at Benson. "Why didn't you come to me first?"

"I did but you wouldn't listen," replied Benson, shrugging his shoulders and turning away from his boss.

"You think you're so clever, don't you, Benson?" Chalk continued. "Well, let me tell you this. You'll find nothing following those fanciful ideas of yours. So carry on and spend your time chasing up children's fantasies, and in the end you'll come back to my way of thinking and you'll wish you'd taken notice of me instead of getting me taken off the case. Because, Benson, the Super will see that you've overreached yourself and that you've conned him, and he'll be begging me to come and take the case back."

Benson kept on looking down at his desk and the video, until Chalk ended his bitter tirade and his accusations and left the office. At which point Benson summoned his new assistant, DC Moore.

"Toby," he said, "can you get your car around to the front, please. We're going to see that girl again. Amy... the one who took this video."

At Amy's house Benson and Moore found her in the middle of a blazing row with her mother. They could hear Amy's voice loud and clear as they made their way up the path to the front door.

"I'm fed up of you," she said. "How many more times do I have to tell you. Stay out of my life. Get off my back and leave me alone. I hate you!"

Mrs Tallon opened the door to Benson's knock, with tears visible in her eyes.

"Oh," she said, "I didn't expect you to be back. I was… er… I was just peeling some onions in the kitchen."

Benson looked at her pityingly.

"Do you want to come in?" asked Mrs Tallon.

"It's Amy we want to see," said Benson softly.

In the house they found Amy to be at her least cooperative and unreasonable best, but she did calm down as they patiently sipped on the tea provided by Mrs Tallon.

Amy couldn't remember anything significant about her time with the Soul Snatcher other than what she'd provided before, but Benson was pleased to see that she did still remember and that she was holding on to a little bit of hope.

"How are things?" he asked Mrs Tallon on the way out.

She gave a forced smile and sighed.

"OK, I guess," she said. "Considering what she went through, but in reality it's very hard. We row all of the time and she's always falling out with people at school and with the neighbours too. Her friends don't come round anymore and I'm getting sick of all the phone calls I keep getting from school about her bullying other pupils and being rude to teachers. To top it all her dad has disowned her, so she no longer goes to see him which means I'm stuck with her in the house all the time when she's not at school.

"To be honest I'm glad when bedtime comes around, at least she doesn't argue and shout in her sleep."

Mrs Tallon choked back her tears.

"I just want my Amy back," she cried. "The real one, not the one who's in there now. You know, every night I pray for her to return. Do you think I'll ever get my prayers answered?"

Benson gave her a sympathetic smile.

Mrs Tallon took his hand.

"Will you find out what's happened to her and will that bring her back to me?" she said pleadingly to Benson and Moore.

"We'll do our best to find out who's done this to Amy," said Benson, touching Mrs Tallon lightly on the arm. "But whether that will make any difference to Amy, who knows?"

"Poor woman," said DC Moore as they walked back to the car.

"Poor Amy," said Benson.

"I'm not sure about this," said Mrs Stewber, eyeing Benson with a mix of suspicion and distrust. "I have to safeguard these children, and what you're asking seems to place them at risk. I'm sorry but I can't agree to this at all."

"I can see where you're coming from," agreed Benson. "But we seriously believe that other children will be taken from this school, and the likelihood is that they'll go for children from the CAB group as they meet after school and whoever or whatever has been taking children from there will continue to do so. There is a firm pattern emerging and we believe it will be repeated."

"If you can get the parents' permission then I'll go along with it, but reluctantly," said Mrs Stewber, offering Benson a compromise, which he eagerly grabbed.

"Fair enough" was his stoical and solemn reply, but inside he was happy.

Two days later the CAB group met. The members logged on to their computers and got about their business as usual. The big difference this time, however, was that each child had a small tracking device attached to some insignificant, and hidden, part of their clothing.

Benson was convinced that the video taken by Amy was genuine. He was equally convinced that another child from the CAB group would be abducted, and he wanted to be able to follow them to wherever they were taken.

It hadn't been easy. He'd had a difficult time persuading the Superintendent of the value in equipping each child with the latest police and security services tracking devices, first because of the cost and secondly because of the fact that Benson was clearly expecting another child to be taken and that wasn't what the Superintendent wanted to hear.

However, Benson had a compelling argument at hand, telling the Superintendent that if his idea bore fruit then he could solve the case and not only get the government off the Super's back, but the Super would get a great amount of kudos for himself and his police force.

Convincing the children's parents had been a lot more difficult. No parent wanted to hear that their child might be the next one to disappear, but Benson pointed out that every child who had disappeared had come back, even though they were different in some way. He told them he was sure more would go and that if the children had tracking devices they could be followed and this could enable the police to intervene before any lasting damage was done to the child. Benson's argument eventually won the day and so every child in CAB was now suitably "wired up".

Benson sat at the back of the classroom as the children laughed, chatted and worked on their projects. His thoughts were wandering and he fought to bring them back into focus, but somehow he couldn't completely get rid of the scenario in his head where he was facing up to his Superintendent after being proved wrong and having several more missing children and a load of very irate parents on his case.

The clock on the classroom wall ticked on and as it did so Benson's vision continued to torment him. With every tick of the clock the imaginary scene in his head became closer to reality. Benson's mouth was dry. He reached for the water bottle on the table in front of him.

At the far end of the room a crowd of children were gathering. There seemed to be some kind of commotion. Benson raised himself from his seat. As he did so a shout went up from the gathering.

"Look out," someone yelled, "Amir's going."

As Benson moved towards the group he could see Amir beginning to sway in his seat. He saw Amir's hands shake as he reached out to the keyboard. Then he saw Amir disappear.

Benson rushed up to the now empty seat, pushing through the small crowd. He looked at the computer screen. In the bottom corner he saw a tiny movement. Peering intently towards the movement, Benson saw a miniature figure wearing a Hoblues blazer. Benson quickly grabbed his mobile phone and switching to camera he began rapidly snapping away at the screen, before swiftly switching back to phone and then ringing his colleague.

"Toby," Benson said urgently as his call was answered. "We're in business! Get the tracking locator up and running. I'll be there as soon as I can!"

CHAPTER THIRTEEN

Back in his office Benson could scarcely contain his excitement. He'd been proved right on the first part of his theory. Now all he needed was to follow up and end this crime.

He had transferred the photographs he took on his phone on to his computer and enlarged them. The prints now blutacked to his office wall confirmed that the figure in the corner of the computer screen was Amir.

The phone rang. Benson picked up. It was DC Moore.

"We've got a location, Sir," he said excitedly. "It's on the Burntbank Industrial Estate."

Benson rushed down to the control room. On his arrival he was met by DC Moore.

"It looks as if it's one of the warehouses there, Sir," he said, pointing at a location on a map that was spread across his desk.

"There are a lot of warehouses on that estate, Toby. Can you be more specific?" asked Benson.

"Not at present, Sir," Moore replied. "But we do know it's on the end of what looks to be the last row. We're trying to find the exact location of that row, and who owns or rents the warehouse."

Benson looked at the tracking screen, then turned to a young constable at a nearby desk.

"PC Hoskins, go and find me the plans for those warehouses. They should give us all the details we want."

He saw a puzzled look on Hoskins' face and added, "call the Town Hall Planning Department and ask them to email a copy to us as a matter of urgency."

Hoskins rushed off and Benson shook his head. "What are they teaching them at police training college these days?" he sighed. A nearby sergeant grinned and nodded in agreement.

After about ten or fifteen minutes Hoskins returned with a printed copy of the plans for the industrial estate.

"Stroll over and get them, did you?" asked the wizened old sergeant sarcastically. Benson frowned at the sergeant before reaching out and taking the copy from Hoskins.

"Thank you, Hoskins," he said.

Benson spread the paper on the desk in front of him and smoothed it down. His eyes followed his finger as it moved swiftly across the page, tracing the outline of the warehouses, before jabbing down firmly on the paper.

"There," said Benson loudly. "That must be the one. It's on the end of the last row."

His eyes swivelled to take in the readings from the tracker that was showing on his computer screen, then quickly swung back to the paper plans.

"That's odd," said Benson.

"What's odd, Sir?" asked WPC Montford.

Benson scratched his head. Then he brought his hand down the front of his face in a gesture of bewilderment and exasperation.

"The tracker doesn't match with the map references on the plans," said Benson. "In fact it doesn't match with any of the warehouses. It's about two or three hundred yards away from the nearest one."

"Surely there's some mistake?" said DC Moore. "Unless the children are being held in the open."

"No," replied Benson. "They're definitely held inside, and it looked like a warehouse on Amy's video. So why is it not there?"

"Perhaps whatever it is that happens to the children takes place in a warehouse but when they first disappear they are held somewhere else, like a temporary shed or recently constructed small building."

The words came from WPC Montford, who immediately regretted intervening in the discussion between senior officers.

"Sorry, Sir," she added, apologetically.

"Possible I suppose," Benson mused. "Good thinking, WPC Montford."

The WPC blushed slightly and gave a bashful grin. "Thank you, Sir," she muttered coyly.

"We'll get a helicopter photo shot," said Benson decisively. "That way we'll be able to see what smaller buildings have been added, or what else might be there. I'll get on to it right away."

"Won't a helicopter flying overhead alarm them, Sir?" asked Moore.

"Maybe, but it's a chance I'll take. The industrial estate isn't that far from the airport so they must be used to having aeroplanes and helicopters flying around for much of the day anyway," countered Benson. He picked up the phone.

"Traffic please," he said.

An hour later Benson and his colleagues were studying aerial pictures of the industrial estate and warehouses, which had just been taken by the crew of the police traffic helicopter.

"There's nothing there," said the sergeant. "Just warehouses, so they must be out in the open somewhere. But there's no field or anything either, so they must be on the concrete or tarmac. Somewhere in that area I'd say." He pointed a wrinkled finger towards a space just beyond the last row of warehouses, at an expanse of land that was visible on the picture.

Benson showed his disappointment by tutting. He had been certain that he would find something in the aerial photos. He was equally certain that the children were not being held in the open. The video had been taken indoors, in a warehouse, of that he was sure. Besides, it didn't make sense to have them outside. If you are going to take something from a child's brain then whatever you take is likely to be valuable, and if it is valuable you want to protect it. So surely you would not want to keep them outdoors where any adverse weather conditions could contribute to illness or malaise in your precious cargo. In any case if you held a child, or children, outside, then anyone could see them and report it, so you wouldn't want to risk that either.

Benson looked at the photograph again, then at the plans, then back to the photograph. He did this for the next ten minutes.

"The same, just warehouses," he thought. "But what am I missing?"

He stared at the plans once more. "Just warehouses," he said quietly. Then he peered at the photographs. "Just warehouses," he repeated, but this time something was stirring ever so slightly in his brain.

"Warehouses... just warehouses... But something is different. What is it?" he mused.

Benson pulled the plans alongside the photos until they were as close as they could be. He traced his finger over both.

"There!" he shouted triumphantly. "There... Look."

He suddenly began counting, "One... two... three... four" and finally "twelve".

Then "One... two... three... four", this time he finished on thirteen.

"Got you!" he yelled.

As the others crowded around Benson pointed to the plans.

"Look," he said. "If you count the number of warehouses there are twelve."

Everyone was counting with him. Then he pulled the photographs towards him.

"Now count the warehouses on the photo," he urged.

There was a pause as everyone counted the warehouses pictured in the aerial photograph.

"Thirteen," came the chorus as they finished.

"Yes," said Benson. "Thirteen. That means one has been added since the plans were drawn up. I'd say that one there."

He jabbed a finger on to the photograph, indicating a building that was a little way from the others on the last row.

"But how could that be?" asked DC Moore. "Surely you need planning permission before you can build something as big as that?"

"And," added DC Wicklow, "building a big warehouse like that without planning permission is hardly something you can hide, unlike a garden shed or a house extension. It must have taken quite a lot of men and a whole load of materials to build that, so people working in the other warehouses would have seen what was going on."

"Hoskins," cried Benson.

"Yes, Sir?" asked Hoskins.

"Go and call the Planning Department and ask them if there has ever been an application to build an additional warehouse on that site, and if so who was it? Also ask how many warehouses they have registered there… And do it quickly please."

Hoskins disappeared from the room, returning ten minutes later to say,

"There have been no further planning applications since the original plans were drawn up, Sir, and the clerk said there are twelve warehouses registered on the site and the last time they were inspected, which was about six months back, there were only twelve."

"There we go then," said Benson jubilantly. "Whatever the extra warehouse is, and however it got there, that's our target. That's where the children are being taken and that's where someone, or something, is performing operations on them."

Benson picked up the phone and dialled an internal number.

"Right, Sergeant," he said into the mouthpiece. "You can get the men assembled for briefing. We've got a location and we're going in."

CHAPTER FOURTEEN

Back at Hoblues High School, Zoe, Simran, Daniel and the rest of the CAB group sat listening to Benson as he gave instructions to his men outside the warehouse. Benson had no idea that his words were being conveyed across the airwaves to the school. He was wearing one of the latest police communication devices that allowed the policemen waiting outside to hear what was happening and to take their cue for action from that.

What Benson wasn't aware of was that because of the link between the warehouse and the school, via the computer system technology used by the Soul Snatcher to abduct pupils through the computer screen, any telecommunication gadget used in the close vicinity to the warehouse could transmit words and conversations into Hoblues' computers.

Simran had been idly flicking through computer programmes and sites when a familiar voice had emerged from the speakers.

"That's that policeman... What's his name?" she heard Zoe say.

"Policeman?" asked Simran. "Who do you mean?"

"You know... that detective... the one who came to talk to us after Amy came back... the one who gave us those tracking thingies... Benyon?... Benton?... " Zoe struggled to find the right name.

"Benson," said Simran.

"That's him," said Zoe. "Let's have a listen and see what's going on. It might be something to do with the Soul Snatcher."

They did listen, and heard Benson tell his men to wait outside and to only go in if he called them or if they felt the situation was desperate or dangerous and he'd not got control of it.

"I'm going in on my own to try to find out what's going on and see how many people are in there," Benson said. "You all know what to do so keep on listening."

He turned to DC Moore and concluded, "Toby, it's up to you to make the call about when to go in if I can't do it for any reason."

Benson crept up to the warehouse and sidled along the wall of the building. He was looking for a door, or some way of entering the building. He walked around the perimeter of the structure but there was no sign of any door, or even a window. Benson could feel exasperation rising inside him. There had to be a way in.

"Come on, try again, think," he urged himself, but his second forage around the building still didn't reveal any way of entrance.

Benson leaned against the wall, his annoyance etched deeply on his face. He stayed like that for about five minutes, racking his brains to find an answer to his frustrated attempts to get inside the building.

"Is everything all right, Sir?" DC Moore's voice came clearly over his communicator. "What's happening?"

"I can't find a way in," replied Benson.

"Do you want us to come and help you?" asked Moore.

"No, I don't want to alert those inside to the fact that we've got men out here," Benson answered.

Before Moore or Benson could communicate further Benson became aware of a slight noise just a few yards away from him. He crept along the wall in the direction of the sound and to his amazement saw it was a door panel, which was now open enough to allow him to pass through. He wondered briefly why he hadn't noticed it on his previous scours of the building, but such thoughts were quickly lost in his excitement at finding a way in.

"I've found an entrance and I'm going in, Toby," he said, before slipping through the aperture and inside the building.

Once inside Benson felt around the wall for a light switch but again to no avail.

"I'll have to risk using my torch," Benson whispered.

He took the slim pencil torch from his pocket and switched it on. In the thin glow he saw a panel on the opposite wall. Creeping steathily across to it, Benson's eyes scanned the array of switches and buttons illuminated in the narrow torch beam. None of them were labelled.

Benson stood for a while pondering which ones he should touch, then in a moment of decisiveness flicked one of the switches. Immediately there was a low rumbling sound followed by the faint hum of an electric motor. A cooling blast of air surrounded him as he realised he had turned on a fan.

Benson pushed another of the buttons and a light came on at the far end of the building. After he had flicked on a further four switches the building was fully illuminated.

He could see stacking shelves around him, which merely confirmed his view that this *was* some sort of warehouse. As he tiptoed silently and slowly towards the far end of the building he caught a glimpse, in the distance, of what appeared to be an operating table, similar to the ones found in a hospital. However, this one seemed to have a kind of headset, with large earpieces, attached to one end. The headset had a sizeable length of cable which climbed upwards to where it was affixed to a big glass tank, which in turn was suspended from the ceiling. This was held in place by metal fastenings. The tank was empty.

As Benson moved further along the far wall of the warehouse more tanks became visible, none attached to operating tables but all suspended from the ceiling in the same manner. In each of these tanks lightning appeared to be dancing. Benson could clearly see small flashes and sparks leaping animatedly around on the inside of the tanks. There was also a swirling mist, or fog, twisting and billowing around in each one.

"It's like a miniature weather system in a bottle," thought Benson, his curiosity aroused.

At the side of each tank was a glass capsule, rather like the glass lifts you might find in some shopping centres. The capsules were smaller than the tanks but connected to them by two thin transparent tubes.

At first glance the capsules appeared to be empty, but as Benson drew closer and changed angles he could see the fuzzy outline of a dark shape inside each one. It was hard to make out exactly what it was as the capsules were way above his eye line. But to his naked eye, and from that distance, the shapes looked very similar to silhouettes of human beings.

At the farthest point of the building Benson came upon a very large computer screen and keyboard. At first he thought they were 3D images as they loomed outwardly towards him and seemed to envelop him, but he quickly realised this was an optical illusion caused by the angle he was standing to them, and they were in fact hollow.

He saw a door at the side of the computer screen. Opening it he ventured inside. There wasn't much room. It was quite small, a bit like being inside a box or a lift. Benson felt around the back wall and located a switch which he flipped, causing the room to be bathed in an eerie pale blue light. Benson realised that he could now see out through the glass screen. There was nothing there but blackness. His gaze swept back to the inside of the computer where he stood, and looking up he saw a circular disc above his head. It looked like an ordinary ceiling light, but there was no light coming from it.

As Benson stared at the disc he heard a faint hum and was suddenly engulfed by a strange sensation. His body was tingling and he began to feel faint. He looked at his hands and was shocked to see his fingers were beginning to disappear. Gasping for breath Benson tried to move but couldn't. He was helpless as he felt himself being drawn upward towards the circular disc. He closed his eyes and prepared for the collision.

CHAPTER FIFTEEN

When Benson opened his eyes he wasn't inside the room behind the computer screen, he was standing in front of the operating table alongside the glass tanks. He made to step forward but found himself unable to move legs or arms. As far as he could see he wasn't bound by rope or wire, or by anything. He was free, yet he couldn't move.

"Welcome, Mr Benson," said a deep voice from somewhere ahead of him. "I have been waiting for you to arrive."

A tall thin figure, dressed in a white suit, black shirt and white tie, emerged into his vision and stood before him. On his head a white top hat was perched. The figure looked vaguely human.

Benson gasped as he saw it. This was the figure he had seen on the video. Benson struggled in vain to move his arms.

"Holding beam," said the creature, as if reading Benson's thoughts and answering his question before it was asked.

"How did I get here? And who are you?" Benson demanded.

"I brought you here by way of a transporter beam," said the creature. "And in answer to your second question my name is Kazzaar and I am from the planet Zaarl."

"Nonsense," said Benson. "There is no such planet. Who are you really?"

"I am Kazzaar, as I said. You will not have heard of my planet. I have travelled from another universe and solar system to get here," said Kazzaar.

"What is your business here? How did you manage to build this warehouse without anyone knowing? And what have you been doing to our children?" asked Benson, trying to sound calm and confident when he really felt helpless and out of control. He was confused and full of doubt about the veracity of the answer to his previous question.

Despite the fact that he felt this way, and he was unable to move, Benson wanted to keep the conversation going so that DC Moore and the men outside would know what was happening and be able to intervene when the moment was right.

"You have so many questions, Mr Benson. Is that what your policemen on Earth always do… ask questions?"

"We do other things too, like solving crimes and arresting and punishing wrongdoers," said Benson. "And that's what we'll be doing to you. I have a lot of men outside. This building is surrounded so you will not be able to escape."

Kazzaar laughed. "Your men are as helpless as you are at this moment," he said. "They are trapped inside a sealed bubble. Don't worry, they will be able to breathe. Our technology will ensure an uninterrupted oxygen supply inside the bubble."

Benson felt his heart sink at this news, but kept on with his questions. He needed to get as much information from this creature as he could to enable him to find a way to free himself and his men, and to stop the child abductions.

"Do you breathe oxygen like us?" asked Benson, deciding that perhaps the creature was right and he did come from another planet, as he remembered the reference to humans in Amy's video.

"No," answered Kazzaar.

"But you're breathing it now, aren't you?" enquired Benson.

"The reason I am here has nothing to do with breathing," said Kazzaar. "It is about survival... about sustenance... about us finding a crucial ingredient for life.

Our species is dying... our planet is dying. Zaarl used to be such a wonderful place to live. We had two suns, which ensured non-stop daylight and sunshine, and that in turn meant we had a constant supply of a chemical that is vital to our existence."

"What changed?" interrupted Benson. "And what brought you to Earth?"

"Our suns have been dying for some time now," said Kazzaar. "There is not long left before they finally expire and our planet dies with them. Our species is quite adaptable though, so we seek a new home. We are what you humans, especially writers of what you like to call science fiction, refer to as shape shifters. That means we can adapt our shape and language to fit in with any species on any planet. We can change our breathing organs too, to allow us to breathe whatever substance or element that is breathed on the planet we are visiting, but we also need to ensure that we have a regular and ongoing supply of our special chemical."

"So why Earth?" Benson repeated, adding, "If you are, as you say, from another galaxy why come here? This is a long way from your home. There must be hundreds, millions even, of planets much closer to your own."

"We have not just targeted your planet," Kazzaar explained. "We have sent members of our species to many planets in many universes and galaxies. We need to explore everywhere so we can find our ideal replacement planet."

"You say many universes. I thought there was only one," said Benson.

"There are many," replied Kazzaar. "In many different dimensions, more than you would ever understand, and we can travel to them all."

"That must have taken a huge number of your population if you are sending rockets complete with crews to all those places," said Benson.

"No," Kazzaar replied. "There is only one species member on each flight."

"But what about all of the tasks that need to be performed on such a long and arduous flight?" asked Benson. "That would take more than one person… and I know there are others in this building besides you as I have seen them on video footage. They are dressed in dark clothes."

"There is only me," Kazzaar repeated. "The others are automatons, robots, humanoids, whatever you wish to call them. They do a lot of important tasks. Some of these tasks may prove to be dangerous but it is all right for them as they are dispensable. We can just clone a replacement. Also they do not require food and sustenance so they do not use up valuable supplies."

"Do they speak our language too?" Benson queried.

"No, they have no need of language. They are programmed to make certain verbal responses and utterances according to the nature of the task before them, all of which are automatically translated into the language of the host planet," clarified Kazzaar.

"What about the children?" Benson enquired. "Where do they fit into this and why have you been taking them?"

Kazzaar began to explain.

"When I came to your planet it was with the intention of seeking out whether supplies of our much-needed chemical, which we know as ZzP2, were readily available here. My automatons and I tested a whole range of species on your planet, the many different types of species you call animals. We also tested all of your plant genera, before moving on to humans. It was here where we found our biggest success. The adult human showed signs of ZzP2 but not in sufficient quantities to raise our interest. But when we tested your children we found a huge difference. The chemical was again present in all of the children we tested but as with adults, often in insufficient amounts. However, in certain types of your children ZzP2 was there in abundance. We explored further and found that children on your planet who are pleasant, cheerful, kind and helpful produce more ZzP2 than do surly and aggressive ones. In fact, I have calculated that throughout the entire child population of your planet there is enough of this chemical produced to enable our species to live quite comfortably on this place you call Earth."

"What is this ZzP2?" asked Benson. "I've never heard of it."

"It is common only to Zaarl," Kazzaar replied. "But humans produce a chemical in their brain called serotonin, and that is the nearest thing to ZzP2 we have found outside of Zaarl. Serotonin is produced in quantity when humans are in a happy mood and enjoying pleasant experiences. Along with the natural painkilling endorphins you produce in similar circumstances, the combination very closely resembles our ZzP2. In the adult population I tested, I found they did not produce enough serotonin or feel-good endorphins. Your adults all seem to be stressed or depressed and too full of tension and anxiety to be properly happy. They also take lots of other chemicals to make them feel better and this interferes with the production of their natural chemicals."

"What's so different about the children?" asked Benson, now intrigued.

Kazzaar allowed himself a little smile. "The ones who are more positive and happy produce more feel-good chemicals and as they sleep better too they can also produce more of a chemical called melatonin. And whilst in humans this has a calming and soporific effect it gives a boost to members of my species. There is a third human chemical called dopamine which is also produced in the brain, and the amalgamation of all of these three, especially with an abundance of serotonin, makes a far stronger combination. Serotonin and dopamine are actually neurotransmitters and melatonin is an indoleamine, but I see them all as chemicals and the effect is the same for my people and their integration is a real bonus for us as it gives us a blend that with a little fine tuning would comfortably sustain our life forms on your planet."

Kazzaar spread his hands as he continued.

"And as your planet also has the potential for us to live in continuous sunshine, if we select geographical areas wisely, this allied to the varied chemical combinations from your children that we can use offers us a very flexible and suitable substitute home for our people."

"But why take children from schools? And different schools at that?" asked Benson, desperate to keep Kazzaar talking so that any of his force who were not trapped in the bubble could locate his whereabouts through tracking the communicating device he was wearing. He knew that people back at the police station would be listening in to his conversation and they would soon come to his aid, and arrest Kazzaar.

"Why not?" said Kazzaar. "It is an ideal and easy place to find children."

"But how do you know they are suitable?" said Benson.

"We have technology that allows us to access school records, which helps us find those who behave well and are positive," said Kazzaar. "There are also lots of computers in schools, and we need these to bring the children to us. We can bring in any child within range of the school grounds through our link with a school's computer system. It is not so important to return the children to the school when we are finished with them, as we can send them to any place that has a computer nearby."

"Aren't they scared when they come here?" Benson enquired.

"Yes," came the reply.

"Doesn't that affect their feelings of happiness and their positive thinking?" Benson queried.

"Yes. But it isn't really a problem as we can still extract the chemicals produced earlier which are still present in their bodies and as an added bonus we also get to extract high- quality chemicals from the adrenalin produced from their fears," Kazzaar retorted.

"How do you bring them here?" Benson asked.

"There is one due to arrive soon," said Kazzaar. "You may observe."

Benson watched as Kazzaar pushed at a small green button on the table before him and immediately the wall behind the table opened to reveal the large computer screen from where Benson had been transported. Kazzaar pressed another button, an orange one this time, and the screen came alive displaying a list of names. At the top of the screen Benson could see the words Hoblues High School. Below this was a list of names that he assumed were pupils. Kazzaar pointed a finger at the screen and moved it slowly downwards. The blue line across the screen moved in conjunction with his finger, flicking over the names before settling on Aaron Cowper. Kazzaar leaned across to the computer keyboard.

"What are you doing?" asked Benson.

"Highlighting the boy's name on the school roll," Kazzaar replied, smiling mockingly. "Now see what happens if I press the delete button."

He stabbed a long bony finger down on the delete key. Immediately Aaron's name disappeared from the screen.

Benson's heart sank. His imagination ran wild, thinking about the possible fates that could now befall the boy. He was dragged back to reality as Kazzaar spoke again.

"He is here," announced Kazzaar. "The boy is now awaiting my attendance."

"But how do you do that? How does it work?" asked a puzzled Benson.

"Our technology creates a transfer tunnel through the computer link with the school and when that is activated, by depressing the delete key, high-intensity ultrasound waves are transmitted. These waves are far superior to anything you have within your scientific knowledge here on your Earth. They first reduce the size of the life form you are transporting and then break down the molecular structure to enable the creature to pass through solid objects without getting hurt. The molecules are then reassembled once the journey is completed. The spirit, or soul, remains conscious throughout so the creature feels that they are still in their body and are being physically pulled through the computer. It's a bit like time travel, but your people have yet to discover that particular form of transport."

Benson was not only astonished by what he'd just witnessed and heard, in a vaguely appreciative way he was impressed too. It was clever, and so simple. What technology did these aliens have that enabled them to delete people and transport them through the ether into a computer screen? And what else could they do with their vastly superior technical knowledge? He suddenly had the feeling that he might be out of his depth.

CHAPTER SIXTEEN

Benson had an urge to go and see the boy and warn him, but he was held fast by the beam, which restrained his movement more efficiently than any high-security prison. He still needed more answers from Kazzaar though, so he restarted the conversation with more questions for his captor.

"You told me about the chemicals you found in these children, but why send them back as negative and aggressive? Surely they are no use to you like that?" he continued.

"What else would we do?" Kazzaar responded. "We need them to grow up and breed so we get more children for us to feed from."

"Breed? What do you mean, breed?" Benson fired another question at Kazzaar. "I thought your trip was a one-off scouting trip to find a planet where you might find the chemicals to save your species?"

"Yes, and we have now found them," said Kazzaar.

"Then surely you can go now and take what you have with you and leave us to get on with our lives and help these poor children to recover from their ordeal?" asked Benson.

"These are just samples," said Kazzaar. "We have need of two more children before we have completed our work on your planet, and even then we have not collected enough to do anything other than show to our scientists, rulers and leaders that this is a suitable place for us to inhabit. Once they agree on that then they can prepare the fleet."

"Fleet?" queried Benson. "What do you mean by fleet?"

"Our evacuation fleet," said Kazzaar. "We will bring every last remaining one of our species to this planet."

"What for?" yelled Benson.

"To live here, of course," said Kazzaar. "This will be our new home."

"An invasion," gasped Benson, now incredulous, and belatedly realising what Kazzaar had meant when he referred to Earth as suitable for sustaining life and becoming a substitute home. "Are you telling me you are sending a fleet to invade our planet?"

"Not an invasion, an evacuation," corrected Kazzaar. "If it was an invasion we would destroy all of your people. That is not our plan. We aim to let you live. It is our intention to take over and colonise your planet. We will set up our factories and laboratories across your world, so we can extract and transport the chemicals to all of our species. This should ensure the ongoing survival of our species."

"But what of the human race?" asked Benson. "They aren't going to just stand by whilst their planet is invaded and colonised. They will fight you."

"There will be no bloodshed," said Kazzaar, quietly and firmly. "If there is resistance, we will use sonic waves and sensor beams to render your people harmless. They will not be able to fight or to have any aggressive thoughts. The human race will meekly surrender to their masters and will serve us obediently and patiently for ever. Fear not. We will take care of you, make you comfortable and look after you. We will wipe out disease from your planet. There will be no famine or war. We will farm the human race for your chemicals. The aggressive and uncaring nature of your children after we have extracted the chemicals will not bother us. If they become too aggressive we will sedate them, and they will still grow up to produce other children for us to ensure a plentiful supply of chemicals for generations to come."

"But why take everything from them?" pleaded Benson. "Why take all the positives and leave them with nothing? Surely a little bit of happiness wouldn't hurt. It wouldn't take too much of your precious chemical from you… and it would encourage them to grow into more positive adults and produce happier children, so you win all round."

"We do leave them a little," argued Kazzaar, somewhat defensively. "In humans there is a feeling called hope, which brings about a general mood of well-being and optimism. This is good for us as it can increase production of those chemicals that are favourable to our existence. However, in my experiments I have found that in many humans hope runs quite shallowly. Your people hope for lottery wins and other easy ways of getting money. Even many of your children hope for material gain in this way, either that or for nothing more than Xboxes or other inane technical gadgetry. That is when they are not hoping to become footballers or singers or other celebrities.

"Such narrow thinking fails to stimulate the brain sufficiently in its manufacturing of feel-good chemicals and so tends to have a limiting effect on their production. The quality of any chemicals induced in this manner is inferior to that which we require. Our species cannot ingest or use this substandard chemical mix, so as our vessels are also organic living creations we programme them to receive and use the inferior substance generated by this type of hope in any way they can to help fuel the long journeys they undertake.

"We need to take care though, as hope is also very important to the human manufacture of feel-good chemicals and without hope human beings tend to live in a state of despair, which often leads to depression. This too adversely affects their chemical production so we have to get the balance right between too much and too little hope, and by allowing humans to keep most of their feelings of hope we ensure that they continue to manufacture the chemicals we need.

"We also need to make certain that we prevent our vessels from getting an overdose of hope. It is dangerous for them if the quality is too rich or the quantity too high. To prevent this from happening, our computer systems are programmed to recognise even the word hope, and to filter it out so it cannot get into the system without approval and so cause confusion by creating the illusion that our spacecraft fuel and energy levels are at critical overload. If the levels did get to that point then the emergency self-destruct procedures would automatically operate by overriding all other controls.

"The filtering system operates at all times except during extraction procedures. This is when we extract the chemicals from the children, at which time all energy and resources are focused on this action.

"You may wonder why I am telling you this. It is because I need you to see that we do not wish to do any permanent harm to your children or to your planet."

Kazzaar smiled languidly, before concluding:

"Besides, you cannot do anything to stop me because by the time you and your other policemen are released from captivity I will be back on my own planet and the evacuation fleet will be on its way here. And if you are able to talk to your superiors before we get here, who will believe you anyway?"

"But aren't you worried that if you leave our children with hope, it will grow and they will eventually destroy you?" asked Benson, searching desperately for an Achilles heel in this alien race.

"No," came the reply from Kazzaar. "Because the rest of their emotions will be negative, and hope will not flourish inside negativity. Hope will merely serve to convince them that they are enjoying their miserable lives and they will lack the confidence, motivation and self-awareness to use their hope positively to improve their lives. Hope on its own is just hope. It is only when hope is accompanied by a will and determination to succeed that motivation increases to a point where it becomes an actuality or achievement. Anyway, even if the children used their hope against us they have so little it would not cause us a problem."

"How do you power your vessels on hope?" Benson was eager to find some weakness he could exploit.

"Our vessels convert the energy from the emotion into a liquid or gas. They can work on either, but the mixture is too rich on its own so they blend it with other fuel sources. We have saved enough hope to use for our return journey. Any more would be dangerous for our vessel so we let the children keep it."

"You talk of a vessel. Did you come to our planet in a spaceship?" asked Benson.

"I came in a transporter," said Kazzaar.

"What, like that beam that brought me here?" Benson enquired.

"No, it is a vessel that travels through space," said Kazzaar.

Benson stared at him for a while. He was about to ask where he had left his space vehicle when the penny dropped.

"This... this building... it is your space ship... but how?" he asked.

"We are shape shifters," replied Kazzaar. "And so are our vessels. But come, we are wasting time. I must attend to the child who has just arrived."

He gestured to one of the automatons to go, and minutes later the child appeared, ushered in by the dapper-looking humanoid who uttered the words, "You will come with me."

Unable to move from the invisible bars that held him prisoner, Benson watched helplessly as the young boy Aaron was marched towards the operating table by Kazzaar's humanoid.

CHAPTER SEVENTEEN

The robot stopped at the edge of the table.

"Lie down on the table, please," said Kazzaar.

"What for?" asked the boy boldly.

"You do not ask questions. You just do as I say," said Kazzaar emotionlessly, as he undid the straps at the side of the table.

"Why should I?" demanded Aaron, adding: "Who are you to give me orders?"

"You do not ask questions," repeated Kazzaar. "You will lie on the table as requested."

"NO, I won't," shouted Aaron defiantly.

Kazzaar motioned to the humanoid who had escorted the boy to the table. The humanoid moved to the boy's side and reaching out an arm he extended a finger, pressing it gently against the lad's neck. Aaron slumped forward but before his body hit the floor it was deftly caught by the humanoid, which calmly and effortlessly lifted the now unconscious child on to the operating table.

Kazzaar swiftly freed the final strap and then expertly secured the boy's frame to the table top.

Benson struggled to find a weakness in the invisible beam that held him so he could help the boy, but there was none and he remained fast in his cell. He had no option but to be an unwilling spectator as Kazzaar attached the large headphones to either side of the boy's head.

Kazzaar plugged the pin that was fixed at the loose end of the headphones into a socket on a small rectangular box which had several dials along its front panel. This box was connected, by a long transparent tube, to one of the empty glass tanks. Kazzaar flicked a switch and the box hummed into life. A light appeared inside the box. The fingers on each of the dials began to flicker and move. Aaron began to stir. He opened his eyes and Benson could see the terror in them as the headphones crackled and pulsated, causing the veins at the side of Aaron's temple to throb rapidly.

Benson reluctantly dragged his eyes away from the boy to look at the tube and tank. The tube shook as it slowly filled with a vapour that had the appearance of steam although Benson was convinced it was something more sinister. The tank began to fill up with this substance, and Benson could see sparks and tiny flashes of lightning leaping and darting about inside the glass.

"What is that inside the tank?" asked Benson.

"That is the soul. The very essence of the chemicals we require," Kazzaar replied. "It will be held in the tanks, in both vapour and liquid form, until we get back to our planet. But we must keep it fresh so it maintains the full nutritious value we require. That is why each tank has a hologram inside it, of the child to whom the soul belongs. Technically the soul is still connected to the child through our computer system until we terminate the link by obliterating the hologram. When we do that, which will be just before we take off to return to our home, the souls we have will become ours and will remain untainted for the journey until we get back to Zaarl where they will be tested again and then used by our people."

"Why take their memories?" Benson enquired.

"We only take the memory of what happened here. It may be too upsetting for the child to remember and that may interfere with their future health and ability to produce healthy children."

"But the children I have spoken to can't remember much about their past," said Benson.

"That is only temporary," stated Kazzaar. "Memories of things that happened before their souls were removed will return but they will be blighted by negativity, and as I said they will never remember what happened to them here."

Benson glanced back at Aaron, whose head was now lolling from side to side as his lips parted, emitting a low moan as they did so.

"Stop it," yelled Benson. "Can't you see what it's doing to him?"

"He is in no pain," said Kazzaar. "The machine is merely extracting his soul. There will be no permanent damage and he will be able to function as normal for the rest of his life."

"Yes," said Benson sadly. "But without his memory or his feelings."

"On the contrary," Kazzaar said. "He will have memory *and* feelings, just not the same as he has now. But he will survive. He will learn to adjust and cope. That is what you humans do. You cope. You survive. Whatever hardship and problems life throws at you, you still survive. You might complain and moan and you might live a life that is less than you would wish it to be, but somehow you get on with it and you pull through. The boy will be no different. We have taken what we want from his soul but we have left him with his negative traits and feelings. Oh, and a little bit of hope too and this will keep him going. In a few years when he has grown into a man he will possibly father a few children and that is good for us as we will be ruling your planet by then, so we will be able to take the good things from his children's souls too."

"You won't get away with this," said Benson angrily. "Someone will stop you."

Kazzaar smiled. "No one will stop us," he said. "Within seven of your days we will be back on our own planet with the samples we have taken from your children. Then within one of your months we will be once more in your world, but this time as rulers. We will be in complete control of your planet."

"You will never reach Earth again," said Benson defiantly. "Your spacecraft will be intercepted and destroyed by our weapons. All of our governments will unite and work together to stop you. We have warning systems and weapons that are there to protect us from any threat from the skies."

"We know all about your warning and weapons systems," Kazzaar replied, smiling. "They are only toys compared to ours. Our technology is far beyond your imagination," He paused before continuing. "Did your technology detect my craft when I arrived? No, it didn't. Why do you think that was, Mr Policeman?"

"I don't know," Benson huffed. "Perhaps because you were alone and they didn't see you as an invader... who knows?"

Kazzaar smiled again, the smug, self-satisfied smile of someone who knows he has won the game. Then he spoke in a calm, assured voice.

"They didn't detect me because our craft have such superior technology that we are undetectable. You people on Earth have spent years developing stealth bomber aircraft that cannot be detected by radar, but our scientists have developed machines that are undetectable by any defence systems on any planet. Besides as I've told you before, we are shape shifters and so are our spacecraft. We can become anything we want to be, as you can see from the fact that my ship has become a warehouse to blend in with the surrounding area. I entered your Earth's atmosphere by adapting the shape of my vessel to become something similar to one of your airliners, but when we have our entire fleet we can be aeroplanes, air balloons, flocks of birds, low cloud, or even raindrops. So even if you had the radar or tracking equipment to find us, we could just keep changing our shapes and our substance to avoid discovery. No, Mr Policeman, you will not stop us and soon we will be the farmers and you will be our livestock."

"Do all of your species look like you?" asked Benson, imagining that if they did, then once they had breached Earth's security systems and assumed their natural state, they would be easy to identify, and possibly to repel.

"No," replied Kazzaar. "This is the shape that I have chosen for my visit here."

Benson's vision faded quicker than a dream on awakening, but he didn't want to show his disappointment to Kazzaar.

"If you don't mind me saying so you don't exactly look like the average human being," smiled Benson.

"I don't need to," said Kazzaar calmly. "I am inside my own spacecraft where no one can see me, so I can be any shape I want, and at the moment I like this one."

"I don't believe you are a shape shifter," said Benson defiantly. He had decided he would try to get Kazzaar angry by challenging his control.

He couldn't really see how it would help his cause, but it just might make him feel a little better if he could score a minor victory over this self-assured and clearly higher-order thinker.

Kazzaar stared haughtily at Benson. He did not speak or blink. Then he closed his large black eyes and stood stock still as if concentrating.

As Benson watched, Kazzaar became a lion, then a snake, then a small terrier dog, and as if to demonstrate that he *could* become a human he became Aaron, the boy on the operating table. Benson looked quickly back and forth from the boy to Kazzaar. They were exactly the same.

Benson was impressed, but also scared. "Is there anything he can't become?" he asked himself. As if to answer his unspoken question Kazzaar changed shape again. This time Benson was shocked to see he was staring at himself.

"OK, OK, I'm convinced," he said loudly. "You can stop now."

Kazzaar reappeared as himself. "As I was saying, Mr Policeman, we can be any shape we want, so your Earth technology will not detect us and neither will your people."

"What about us?" Benson asked. "You can't keep us here until you leave. We will be missed and someone will come looking for us."

"They will not find you," said Kazzaar casually. "And as for your colleagues trapped outside in my bubble, they will not be seen either as the bubble is also designed to blend in with the shape of its surroundings. It will look like an extended part of the outside wall and no one can see inside it. And just in case you are thinking that they may already have used their radios to call for help, I can tell you that the bubble, like this spacecraft, is both sound and radio wave proof. No sound can be transmitted to the outside world unless it goes through the computer link, and as that link is not open to the world you will not be heard."

"What are you going to do with us when you leave," asked Benson. "Kill us?"

"We are not killers," said Kazzaar. "We will release you. But not before we have wiped your minds of all of these events. Do not worry, you will still retain your memories but not of us or our intentions."

CHAPTER EIGHTEEN

The CAB members had sat in silence listening to the conversation between Benson and Kazzaar. Now Zoe spoke.

"We've got to do something," she said. "That thing, the Soul Snatcher or whatever it is… it's going to leave soon and once it does it will take the souls of all of those children and go back to its own planet. Then when the people… or things… that live there see how good those souls are for their survival they'll all come down here and take over the Earth, and we're the only ones outside of that warehouse who know this." Zoe smiled, and then said, "We do have one advantage though."

"What's that?" asked Courtney.

"The Soul Snatcher thinks that as his spaceship or whatever it's called is sound and radio wave proof, no one can hear his conversation with Benson… but he's wrong. We can hear him because of the direct computer link with his ship."

"But what can we do?" asked Simran despairingly. "We're miles away from where the action is and if we tell the police what we've heard no one will believe us. Besides, even if we went to the warehouse how can we possibly fight that thing?"

"Haven't you been listening?" said Zoe tetchily. "The Soul Snatcher said that they couldn't deal with hope. Somehow we have to find a way of exploiting that weakness. So I'd say that right now we could do with a whole lot of hope, along with a way to use it to beat that thing."

"And just how do we get that?" asked Harjoyt gloomily. "It's not as if they sell it in shops, is it? Where do we get hope from? And how much is enough?"

"Oh, I don't know," growled Zoe. "It's just a thought. Come on, everyone. Think! We need to try to figure out how we can use that information to destroy the Soul Snatcher and save our planet."

The room returned to silence as everyone tried hard to think of a way they could find a solution that would help them save the Earth and get everything back to normal.

Suddenly Zoe gave a whoop of delight.

"I think I might have got it," she said triumphantly. "This computer system is a star network system."

"So what?" moaned Harjoyt.

"So we can attune every computer in the room to this one," said Zoe. Then looking around the room she said:

"OK, everyone keep on watching and listening. I'm going into that warehouse."

"You can't go in, you'll be seen and trapped in one of those bubbles before you get inside," said Simran.

"Not if I go in through the computer," Zoe responded.

"How will you do that?" asked Harjoyt.

"Not sure yet," said Zoe. "But if my thinking is correct I will have the answer any time now. Does anyone remember which computer Ella was sitting at when she was pulled into the screen?"

Daniel pointed to a computer near to him. "It was this one," he said.

"Are you sure?" asked Zoe.

"Yes," said Daniel. "Because Amy was talking to her at the time and I was sitting right here, where I am now."

"What about Amy?" asked Zoe. "Where was she sitting when *she* disappeared and which computer was she using?"

"The same one," said Courtney. "We were sitting together if you remember, and as you shouted 'Look at Amy' I saw her in the screen. That one there, the same one as Ella went into."

"Right, everyone, I want you all to attune every computer in this room into the site I've got on mine. You know the one. It's where we are connected to the warehouse. When you do that you should get a list of Hoblues pupils on your screen."

When everyone had done this Zoe summoned Simran to her side. Then turning to the others she said:

"If I'm right that must mean that this computer is the main one. The one currently connected directly to the Soul Snatcher and with a passage to the inside of the warehouse."

"So?" queried Daniel. "What does that prove?"

"Nothing," replied Zoe. "But it gives me a chance of getting into the warehouse without being seen."

"How?" asked Courtney.

"The same way as the others," answered Zoe. "You heard the Soul Snatcher say that he highlights names on the school roll and then presses the delete key. Now, Simran, when I've gone I want you to find the ICT technician and get him to direct all output from every computer in this room through the main one straight away."

"Why?," asked Simran.

"So we can be sure that anything we send will go straight to the warehouse computer," said Zoe.

"What are we going to send?" asked Harjot.

"Enough stuff to save the planet," said Zoe enthusiastically. She turned back to Simran. "Don't forget. Ask the technician to direct everything into this computer."

"But what if it can't be done?" asked Simran.

"Then we're in big trouble. But we'll just have to hope that if we can't do that then we can get the same message to the warehouse from individual computers," said Zoe. "Either way I won't be able to do anything as I'll be with the Soul Snatcher, because I'm going to highlight my name on this computer, press delete and see if it takes me into his lair."

"WHAT?" There was a chorus from everyone in the room. "Are you mad? Why?"

"Because I think I've found a way to defeat him," said Zoe.

"How?" asked Daniel.

"With hope, as I said before" was Zoe's answer.

"Will it work?" asked Courtney.

"Don't know," said Zoe, shrugging her shoulders. "But we know hope can be dangerous to the Snatcher and if you remember the legend of Pandora's Box, then you'll also remember that hope was all that was left in the box after all the ills and evils had flown out and invaded the world, but the world still survived. So let's work on the basis that hope will do the same here."

She turned to Simran.

"Keep these computers tuned to that site, stay listening in, and this is what I want you to do when the time is right, but only when you hear me tell you to do it."

Zoe whispered something in Simran's ear. She then scrolled down the names on the default computer screen until the blue cursor line highlighted her own name. She pressed the delete button, swayed back and forth on her chair for a brief moment, then lurched towards the computer screen, turning briefly to wave goodbye to the gaping onlookers before plunging through the glass.

The journey through cyber space was uncomfortable for Zoe as, unlike the others before her, she was conscious of it. She had no idea what to expect at the other end but she was alert to any possibility. The most important thing for her was not to be discovered. If she was, then that was the end of her plan and she didn't want to think what might happen to her and to planet Earth.

When she arrived in the inner room of the computer inside the warehouse, Zoe immediately saw the ceiling light above her head. She didn't know what it was but she had already decided to avoid anything that might look as if it could trap or transport her, or alert anyone to her presence in the building. Zoe thought the light might be a security camera so she kept to the sides of the computer wall, giving the circular disc a wide berth.

Zoe soon located the door and stepped out into the warehouse. The place was bathed in light, which immediately filled her with alarm, but she thought, "If I keep to the edges where those racks are, I can maybe get down to where the Soul Snatcher is without anyone seeing me."

Quite how she would do what she planned to do, if she did get there, Zoe had not yet thought out. She would just play it by ear, but she did hope to be able to free Benson from the beam that held him and maybe he would take over and that would enable her to put the plan she had arranged with Simran into action.

Zoe inched her way along the racks, keeping to the shadows. Already she could see the operating table ahead of her. She could also see the Soul Snatcher. He had his back to her as he stood before Benson who was locked inside his invisible prison.

As she got nearer Benson caught sight of her and lifted his head. He opened his mouth as if to speak. Zoe placed a finger on her lips to motion him to keep quiet. She then opened and closed her mouth rapidly while at the same time waving her fingers in a gesture suggesting he keep on talking to his captor. She mouthed the words, "Ask him more about hope."

After two or three attempts she finally got Benson to interpret her mime and understand what she wanted. "Phew," she thought when he indicated his understanding with a nod of his head. "Charades was never this difficult."

Benson, as requested, spoke to the Soul Snatcher.

"Just one point I would like you to clear up," he said. "It's about what you mentioned earlier… about too much hope being dangerous. How does that work then?"

The Soul Snatcher was confident and relaxed. He had his pursuers captured and nothing could stop him now returning to his planet with the message that Earth could be successfully colonised. He saw no problem in answering Benson's question.

"Too much hope would overload the fuel tanks with a mixture that is too rich for them to operate properly," he said smiling. "But I've told you that before."

"Yes, but what would happen in the event of an overload? Would your vessel just be unable to take off? Or would it explode? And if it did explode, it would be a big explosion so wouldn't that damage the planet you were aiming to live on… or at the very least cause panic and an investigation that might alert the authorities to the fact that you'd been here?" Benson asked.

"So many questions, Mr Policeman," said the Soul Snatcher in a voice that was soft but assured. "However, I *will* answer them if just to satisfy your curiosity, as the information will not benefit you in any other way." He smiled again, then continued. "The answer to your question is no. Our vessels do not explode, quite the reverse in fact. They are programmed to implode. So in such an event the vessel would merely collapse in on itself destroying everything within, and leaving no clues and no trace of anyone being here."

"What happens if you don't return home?" asked Benson. "Will others come looking for you? Or maybe come to repeat your experiments?"

"No," came the reply. "If any of our vessels, or people, do not return it will be assumed that we perished on the planet, either because it was unable to sustain the existence of our life form, or because we were killed by hostile inhabitants. But I do not see the purpose in your questions as you cannot do anything to affect this. So enough of this idle chatter, I have one more child to find and then I can leave you and your planet for the time being."

Zoe had been listening to this conversation as she crept ever closer to the pair. She was now alongside the operating table. She ducked down beneath the table as she pondered her next move. Suddenly her arm was grabbed and pulled behind her back. She felt herself in a vice-like grip. A voice from right behind her said,

"You will come with me."

CHAPTER NINETEEN

Zoe found herself in the grip of a dark-suited humanoid, who was pulling her roughly on to the operating table. She tried to resist, fighting with all of her strength to break away. The humanoid stretched out a hand and touched Zoe's neck. Then all went dark.

Zoe awoke on the operating table. The Soul Snatcher stood at her side. He was securing her to the table with what appeared to be leather straps.

"You have saved me a lot of time, my dear," he said. "I no longer have to search for my final child. She has come to me. You are a little bit more feisty and bold than the children I usually look for but that could mean richer pickings for me when I take the chemical products in your soul. Don't look so disappointed, I knew you were in the building from the moment you came through the computer link. I could have activated the transporter beam in the computer but I thought it would be fun to see how far you would get and what you would try to do. I am very impressed that you managed to get as far as you did before my humanoids accosted you, but I am disappointed that you seem to have no plans beyond creeping up on me. No matter, I will take your soul and then I can return to my home sooner than I anticipated. Thank you, my child. You have been very helpful."

"Let me go!" screamed Zoe. "You won't get away with this."

Kazzaar smiled. "They always say that," he said. "But the funny thing is I do!"

Benson watched helplessly as Kazzaar secured Zoe on to the table with the straps. He felt angry at Kazzaar and at himself for allowing himself to be caught and so put this child and the world at risk.

"Leave her alone," he yelled. "Let her go. You must have enough chemical without taking from her."

Kazzaar ignored him. He reached for the headphones to fasten on to Zoe's head. Zoe took the opportunity to turn her head briefly so she could glance at the computer screen. What she saw there lifted her spirits.

"Well done, Simran and CAB," she whispered quietly, permitting herself a faint smile.

"I'm glad you find some amusement in the situation you are in," said Kazzaar, noticing Zoe's smile. "It will mean you are in a happy state when the chemical is extracted so we will get more chemicals."

He placed the headphones at each side of Zoe's head and secured the other end to the socket on the box with dials. Kazzaar gave a little bow in the direction of Zoe and then reached out towards the switch.

"Simran, do it now," yelled Zoe "DO IT NOW!"

Nothing happened. Zoe shouted in the direction of Benson.

"Mr Policeman... Mr... er... Benson is it? Please, quickly shout to Simran to do it now. Please, before it's too late."

Kazzaar had withdrawn his hand from the switch. He turned round to look at Benson.

"What's this about?" he asked. "You think you can stop me? Is that it, child?" He looked at Zoe. "I've told you... you cannot stop me, so please, less of this distraction. I need you to be calm and relaxed."

Zoe was screaming at Benson now. "Do as I ask, please. Simran is waiting on instructions. She can hear what's going on through the computer link. It's picking up the conversation through your communicator. We have a plan to stop this. Go on, tell her to do it! Tell her Zoe says to do it."

Kazzaar leapt across the room towards Benson with the intention of stopping him from speaking, but Benson had decided he would do as Zoe asked, even though he didn't fully understand what she meant. Benson yelled into his communicator at the top of his voice,

"Simran… do it. Simran, can you hear me? Go for it. Do whatever it is that Zoe asked you to do. Do it NOW!"

Seconds later Benson's mouth was covered by a strip of adhesive tape and his arms were immobilised as the pressure of the holding beam was increased.

Realising that the spaceship had a sound link to the school computer, and that this was probably the source of Zoe's request for Benson to communicate with Simran, Kazzaar tore out the communication device from beneath Benson's jacket and hurled it towards one of the robots. The humanoid caught it deftly and immediately crushed it into tiny pieces as his hands made rapid circular movements around the object.

The hand grinding continued until nothing was left of the disc but a fine dust.

Zoe turned her head to look at the computer screen. It was just the same as before. Nothing had moved. Zoe gave a big sigh.

"Well, at least we tried," she said.

Kazzaar laughed loudly as he spoke to Zoe.

"Whatever your plan was, my child, it has not worked. I said you wouldn't be able to stop me and you haven't. You Earth people are powerless against us and whatever you planned has proved to be useless. There is nothing you can do to harm us, so make the best of your time whilst we are away, for on our return we will become masters of the Earth."

Kazzaar reached forward and adjusted the dials on the box in front of him.

"I think we may need a little more power for you," he said to Zoe. "You have more fight and resistance than the others."

He laughed again. "So, my child, say goodbye to your soul. It will make someone very happy back on Zaarl."

His finger flicked the switch and the machine began its rhythmic hum as it burst into life.

Zoe strained and twisted her head in a vain attempt at shaking the headphones loose. Benson watched her struggles with a mix of anger and sadness.

Zoe felt the first impulses pounding her brain. She shook her head and tried to wriggle free from her bonds. The impulses got stronger. She felt her thoughts and memories beginning to disintegrate under the pressure. She could feel them being sucked slowly from her brain. Zoe screamed.

Then all went silent for a moment.

Back in Hoblues School, Simran had heard the command from Benson and given her orders to the CAB members. Children's fingers sped across keyboards at breakneck speed, some rapidly depressing the delete key and scrolling down names in a blur, some typing out the same word over and over again in ever-increasing font size. They listened to the broadcast from the warehouse as they worked. Suddenly there was a loud buzzing and grinding noise and all went quiet.

Everyone sat back and looked at Simran.

"Don't stop," Simran shouted. "We have to carry on as if we still had sound. We must complete what we are trying to do and hope for the best. We won't know whether we have been successful or not but please… don't give up… For the sake of all the children… and the world… we have to keep on."

Everyone did keep on. Fingers settled once more on keyboards and the clatter of noise and rapid fluctuation of words on the computer screens continued, stopping, in part, only when the list of names on the school roll had ended.

"Well done," said Simran to the pupils who had been engaged in this task. "But the rest of you must carry on, and those of you who have finished, you can join the others in their typing."

In the warehouse Benson stared sadly at Zoe's contorted body as it fought against the electric current flooding through her consciousness. Suddenly the sound of a klaxon pierced the low drone of electricity. Lights began to flash on and off on the machine that was siphoning off Zoe's subconscious being, and also on the fascia of the computer screen. The racks, tanks and hoses rattled and shook in unison as a disembodied voice began a countdown. The pressure in Zoe's brain lessened and then stopped altogether.

"Engines in meltdown due to overload, fifteen minutes and forty-six seconds to self-destruction time," it said.

Kazzaar sprinted towards the central control panel of his spacecraft, which neither Zoe nor Benson had noticed before. This was situated at the far end of the operating table in an area that had been in shadow. Now it was bathed in a deep red light that became brighter and then duller as the red lights on the fascia flashed their alternating on/off message.

Kazzaar frenziedly pushed buttons and pulled levers as he tried to correct the fault. But the lights continued to flash and the klaxon blared out its never-ending refrain. His face showed concern. His smooth, slow, soft voice tone and laid-back demeanour disappeared as he frantically tried to put right what he saw as a normal malfunction.

"Abort countdown. Return to operating mode," he yelled into what looked like a microphone. "Do you hear me? Abort countdown and return to operating mode."

"Fourteen minutes and twenty-eight seconds to self-destruction time," came the response from above his head.

Kazzaar ran back to where Zoe lay on the table. She was recovering her consciousness and awareness following the abrupt ending to her terrifying ordeal. She twisted her neck to see the computer screen as Kazzaar approached. What she saw there made her smile broadly.

"What have you done?" Kazzaar asked, his face contorted into a hideous, horrifying mask of rage. "TELL ME WHAT YOU HAVE DONE!"

Zoe kept on smiling. She gave no answer to her tormentor. Kazzaar's fingers fumbled with the straps that held her fast to the table.

"I am releasing you," he said. "Whatever it is that you have done, you will reverse it."

"I don't think so," replied Zoe.

Kazzaar grabbed Zoe's newly freed arms.

"You will do as I say," he ordered. "Or you will be hurt."

"Leave her alone," yelled Benson, suddenly finding his arms free and tearing the gag from his lips. "I thought you said your race were not killers?"

"We are not," Kazzaar replied, and then added cruelly, "But that trait does not extend to our humanoids."

He turned back to Zoe.

"Now," he said menacingly, "reverse this and stop it, or I will summon my androids to tear you apart.

For a moment fear returned to Zoe. She had no wish to have her body torn limb from limb, but then neither did she have any intention of stopping the destruction of the Soul Snatcher and his evil plans. Not that she could anyway as he had destroyed her only way of communicating with Simran and the CAB group.

Kazzaar let go of Zoe's arms. She raised herself up on the operating table until she was in a sitting position. She could, she supposed, stall for time until the self-destruction process was completed. But even if Kazzaar did wait for another fourteen minutes or so without turning the robots loose on her, she didn't want to be in the building when it collapsed. So what was she to do?

The answer presented itself to her very quickly. As the voice announced that there were thirteen minutes and fifteen seconds to go she caught a glimpse of the dark-suited humanoids nearby, but they didn't look to be as full of beans as they were before. The arms and legs on each humanoid were now twitching animatedly and their heads were revolving slowly in a 360 degree circle at the top of their sharp-suited bodies. It looked as if they were some bizarre mechanised dance troupe performing one of their routines. Zoe's fears eased at the sight. She made as if to get down from the table but Kazzaar grabbed her arms once more.

"Are you going to stop this?" he growled.

"No, I'm not," smiled Zoe.

"Well, we'll see if you change your mind when the humanoids begin their work," said Kazzaar, who clearly hadn't noticed that the robots weren't in a suitable condition to carry out his foul orders. He barked out a command.

"Take the girl and eliminate her," he said coldly.

Benson screamed at Kazzaar to let Zoe go and as he did so he too saw the robots. Their twitching and shaking had now become more urgent and so had the revolving heads, which now resembled the spinning blur of a spin-dryer full of clothes. Within seconds the heads burst open and the bodies slumped forward, making a crashing sound as they hit the floor.

Kazzaar looked at them in despair. He still held on to Zoe. Meanwhile Benson felt the physical force around him subside. He moved his feet tentatively, stepping slowly out of his prison cell. The holding beam had perished in the mayhem leading towards self-destruction. Benson leaped forward and grabbed Kazzaar, prising him away from Zoe. As he did so, DC Moore and a group of about twenty policemen and women came running down the aisle towards them. The bubble that had held them prisoner outside had gone the same way as the holding beam, both unable to function under the vessel's self-destruct mode.

CHAPTER TWENTY

"What's going on, Sir?" asked DC Moore. "We've been trapped outside in some kind of transparent tent. We lost contact with your communication device and had no idea where you were or what you were doing. What's happening?… and who is that?"

The last question was asked with Moore pointing at Kazzaar. Then catching sight of Zoe he said, "Why is there a schoolgirl in here?" His gaze settled on the figure of Aaron who was still on the other operating table. "And a boy," he added.

Benson opened his mouth to explain but his voice was drowned out.

"Eleven minutes and thirty-two seconds to self-destruction time."

"What's that about?" Moore asked.

"I'll tell you everything later, Toby," said Benson, his voice urgent. "We need to get out of here quickly."

"We can't go until we've restored those souls to their owners," said Zoe, pointing to the tanks.

"How do we do that?" asked Benson, puzzled. He turned to Kazzaar.

"Can you help?" Benson enquired.

"I could, but I won't," said Kazzaar laconically. "Why should I? You have destroyed my vessel and my humanoids, and now I cannot get home and so my people will be denied the chance to settle on your planet. If my fellow explorers are unable to find another suitable planet for them to live on then they will all die."

"But you have no use for these souls now," begged Zoe. "And these are the souls of children who have yet to live their full lives. They are innocent in all of this. They aren't the ones who have destroyed your ship, it is us and we have only done it to stop you from taking over the Earth. We are defending our planet and our home because that is what we have a right to do if you plan to invade us. *You* are the ones who came here to hurt us. You could have gone anywhere. Found some planet where no one lives, but you came here and decided to take over our world without any thought of how we might feel about that. And anyway you said your people have gone to other planets too, so you obviously don't care about other races, only about yourselves, and what if one of your expeditions do find somewhere suitable? Then your people will live. So you cannot say they will die because of us. Please help these poor children to be reunited with their souls. You may not be able to save your ship, or yourself, but you can save them."

"It is no use," said Kazzaar. "The children are no longer here."

"I heard you say before that technically the soul is still connected to the child through your computer system until you terminate the link by obliterating the hologram," said Zoe triumphantly. "So that means there must be some way of reversing the process and getting them back to the children."

"What a clever child you are," said Kazzaar before he was interrupted by the next announcement.

"Ten minutes and two seconds to self-destruction time."

"Please," Zoe pleaded. "Please save them. They are only children. They don't deserve this. How would you feel if they were your children?"

Kazzaar looked at Zoe's face, screwed up in earnest as she made her pleas, tears glistening in her eyes.

"Because they are children," he whispered softly, "I will help."

He turned to Benson and Moore and added, "But you are adults so you will have to fend for yourselves."

Kazzaar walked across to one of the racks and placed one of his long fingers into a small indentation on the surround, which appeared to be made of a hard plastic-type material. Immediately a panel slid open revealing a second computer and keyboard. Kazzaar tapped his fingers on the keyboard, bringing the screen to life. He selected a programme and a list of names appeared on the screen. Against each name was a picture of a child. Zoe recognised Ella, Amy and Amir straight away, but could not place any of the others. She assumed this was the computer link to the children's souls that were in the tanks. She watched intently as Kazzaar clicked the cursor on to a heading at the top of the screen. A menu box appeared on the screen. The menu gave three choices: Detach/Save – Destroy - Reverse/Return. Kazzaar moved the cursor upwards and clicked on to select all. The names on the screen were all highlighted in blue. He moved the cursor down to the menu box.

Zoe, Benson and Moore watched him closely as he went about the task. Zoe was so close that her face was almost touching Kazzaar's face.

As the cursor moved into the box, Zoe saw Kazzaar's thick black lips part in an evil grin. On the screen the cursor settled on the instruction Destroy. Kazzaar threw his head back and laughed out loud.

"Do you honestly think I would save these souls after you have destroyed the future for the souls on my planet?" he snarled. "I say an eye for an eye. The children's souls will perish, but unlike my people their bodies will live on. Even if they are not as they were, they will still be better off than my people."

Kazzaar's hand made to press the enter key, but Zoe was too quick for him. She nudged him hard with her shoulder, knocking him off balance. Simultaneously her hands moved to the keyboard, swiftly locating and moving the cursor on to Reverse/Return. Her hands rapidly shot across the board and pressed Enter.

Inside the tanks things started to happen. Each tank burst into life. Liquid bubbled, lightning flashes became bigger and more energised, and the covering of steam began to evaporate. The tanks shook as they combined in a routine of mass vibration, causing the attached tubes to engage in an orgy of frenzied animation as they shook, throbbed and pulsed.

"Eight minutes and seventeen seconds to self-destruction time," came the announcement.

The tanks were now in full throttle.

"What's happening?" asked Benson.

"I've no idea," replied Zoe. "I guess they're emptying their contents back into the children, but I don't know how."

"The souls are flying back to the people who gave them," said Kazzaar gloomily. "They are still as they were. We could not cut the connection as we needed to keep them alive and fresh for our journey back to my home... a journey which will not now take place."

"How does it work?" Zoe asked.

"Our technology was able to sustain the connection by using the tanks and the tube connections. The hologram was formed from part of the persona of each child, thus maintaining the link with the child. Technically the souls were always still inside the children, although they were physically here inside the tanks. That is why some memories reappeared in the children and then disappeared again.

"When we extracted the soul we inserted a filter into each child's brain through the headphones. The filter acts to block out certain thoughts and memories, a bit like having something stuck in your ear might block out sounds, and it also changes the way you think and react to people and events.

By the time we were ready to return to our own planet, the children would have grown accustomed to feeling and thinking in that way, so when we broke the connection there would have been no reaction and no recognition of their loss. We would have left Earth with all of the souls intact, but now you have reversed the process the filter is gone and all souls are returned to whoever gave them. The children will be as they were before and they will remember nothing of the event."

"You said earlier that you had converted the souls into liquid form," said Benson.

"Yes, I did," Kazzaar said. "But that wasn't strictly true. It was only the chemicals that the children's brains produced. We needed the souls to remain attached so that the chemicals could maintain their original volume and mass for our homeward journey. That way both our people and our scientists would benefit."

"Six minutes and forty-four seconds to self-destruction time," said the voice.

"We must get out of here," said Benson urgently.

He grabbed Zoe's arm, as DC Moore freed Aaron and urged him to run.

"Where am I and what am I doing here?" asked Aaron. "And come to think of it, who are you?"

He turned to Zoe. "Hi Zoe, what's going on?" he asked.

"Come on," Benson urged Zoe. "You've done all you can now. You can explain how you did it once we get out safely."

"What about him, Sir?" asked DC Moore, pointing to Kazzaar. "Shall I get one of my men to arrest him?"

"No," said Benson. "Leave him here. The warehouse is his spaceship and it's programmed to implode so it will destroy everything that is inside, which includes him."

"Sir?" queried Moore, looking puzzled.

"It's too complicated, Toby," snapped Benson.

Zoe broke free from Benson's hold and looked beseechingly at him.

"You can't just leave him," she argued. "Despite what he's done, he's entitled to a fair trial."

Benson took a deep breath and then answered Zoe's pleas.

"If we arrest him he'll face all sorts of questions from scientists, government officials and everybody else the world over. The media, and Uncle Tom Cobley and all, will want a piece of him. There'll be arguments and fights over who should have custody of him and where he should be held captive. Governments and countries will fall out and wars could be started all because of him. He'd love that, wouldn't he? That would help make up for losing out on what he came here for. I don't want to be the one responsible for putting the world through that, but I don't want to let him go either. I certainly don't want him wandering our planet. Who knows what hidden powers he might have or what he might be able to do to the human race?"

Benson paused for breath. Then he continued as Zoe opened her mouth to intervene.

"He was quite prepared to harm you." He pointed at Zoe. "And he had no qualms about harming all of those other children. Also, he and his people planned to colonise the Earth and turn the human race into robotic slaves. He's captain of this vessel so he can go down with his ship in the good old Earthly tradition."

"But… " DC Moore began to speak.

"Three minutes and six seconds to self-destruction time," the voice announced.

"Don't argue, Toby," said Benson. "We've got to get going. We need to find a way out of here or *we'll* be going down with the ship too."

He turned to Kazzaar.

"Goodbye, Kazzaar," he said. "I'm glad you didn't succeed in your plan and I'm sorry to leave you to your fate, but believe me you wouldn't want to be part of the circus that would take place if we handed you over to the authorities on Earth. You could end up being tortured or dissected and despite what you have done you don't deserve that… Good luck. Whatever happens to you I hope it will be quick so you don't suffer unduly."

Benson turned on his heel, pushed Zoe in front of him and yelled, "Everyone, come on, let's get out of here."

They ran towards the end of the building leaving Kazzaar behind them.

At the end of the warehouse Benson and his men searched frantically for a door or a window that they could use to get out of the doomed spacecraft. Behind them they heard the voice continue its countdown to obliteration.

"One minute and twelve seconds to self-destruction time."

Desperately, the policemen scanned every part of the walls and ceiling in a bid to find the opening that would take them to the safety of the world outside.

"Why didn't one of you notice where the door was when we came in?" DC Moore chided his men.

"We could go back and ask Kazzaar," said a desperate police constable.

"It's too late… we're all going to go with the building," whimpered another policeman, as the fleeing men ran their hands over everywhere trying to locate something that resembled a door or a handle.

A sudden flash of red light illuminated the area briefly as the countdown reached its final critical point before implosion. It was enough to enable Zoe to see the small panel on the wall behind one of the racks.

"There," she cried, pointing.

Benson's eyes followed the direction of her finger. He raced over, reached up and began to feverishly press all of the buttons. Just for good measure he also pulled the side lever.

The spaceship was flooded with white light.

"Damn," said Benson "They're only light switches."

"No they're not," Zoe almost screamed. "Look!"

A small aperture had appeared on the wall in front of them. Beyond it Zoe could see stars and lights twinkling.

"That's not a picture," she gasped. "It's outside… we can get out through here."

Zoe led the way, followed by Aaron. There was a scramble as everyone rushed to get through the tiny gap. Benson was the last one to emerge on the other side. As he climbed through he heard the voice say,"Twenty seconds to self-destruction time."

Once outside everyone ran as fast as they could to get away from the doomed craft. No one knew quite what to expect with the impending implosion and they didn't want to get caught in any shock waves or hit by any stray flying debris.

The men, still led by Zoe, ran until they found a spot they considered to be a safe distance from the doomed spaceship. Then they stood and watched as the construction began to fold in on itself, slowly at first, like a bouncy castle that has sprung a leak, before collapsing inwardly like a house of cards. The final stage came when the spacecraft disappeared altogether. When Benson and Moore went over to look there was no trace of it, not even a speck of dust. It was as if it had never existed.

"Right," said Benson. "I guess we'd better get back. I need to write my report, although I've no idea what I'm going to write. I suppose I'll just have to make something up, and now that the children are all back to normal maybe we can just tell the parents that we've found who was responsible but that he's no longer with us, or say that this was a joke that misfired."

Benson smiled at Zoe.

"You did well in there," he said, nodding towards where the spaceship had once stood. "But I've no idea what you did… or how you got here. Do you want to tell me?"

"Of course," said Zoe. "We picked up your conversation with your men just before you went into Kazzaar's spaceship, or whatever it is, and synchronised our school computers into the one that was here. Then we followed your conversation with Kazzaar on our computer and came up with an idea we thought might stop him. So I decided to send myself here to carry out my part, whilst the others did the rest.

Before I transported myself through the computer into Kazzaar's spaceship I thought about what he'd said about it not being able to cope with a lot of hope. I thought that might be significant so I checked the names of all of the children who had been abducted and guess what? No one who has the name of Hope, either for a first or last name, has ever been taken. I had heard Kazzaar telling you that the computer system was programmed to filter out the word hope except during the chemical extraction process. Even though it was a bit of a long shot I thought this might mean that even the name Hope could affect the overload system on the fuel consumption if it happened during the extraction process, so I took a chance. I decided that as there seemed to be a direct connection between the school roll, with the list of pupils' names on the computer, and the spaceship computer, then maybe if we changed all of the children's names, either first or second, to Hope and send them all through the system then the ship wouldn't cope, and the engines, or whatever, would overload. But I had to make sure that I was on the table at the time so that the extraction programme was in operation, meaning that the filtering system wouldn't be functioning.

So I got CAB members to do just that and I asked Simran to make sure that CAB members highlighted the words and kept on pressing the delete button so that everyone got sent through the computer link until it was flooded with Hope. Just for good measure I also asked the group to keep on typing the word HOPE in bigger and bigger, and bolder, font as many times as they could and send that too.

After you told her to do it, when I was lying on the table, the Soul Snatcher destroyed the sound connection to the computer so I didn't know if Simran had heard the message, but when I turned my head as I was on the table, though it hurt I could see the words coming through on the computer screen. All I had to do then was hope that Simran had heard your final instruction, and to stop the Soul Snatcher from seeing it, after which it was just a question of whether, and how long, it would take for the ship to reach overload."

"You are a genius, girl," said Benson, smiling. "And you've saved the world!"

"Not just me," said Zoe. "It's down to CAB… We've done this together."

She looked earnestly at Benson.

"What do you think happened to the Soul Snatcher?" she asked. "Do you think more of his people will come here? Do you think he might still be alive? How would we know? After all, he said he was a shape shifter."

"I think we've seen the last of him… and his species," said Benson. "So let's get you back home, and tomorrow the world will continue as usual, and long may it last."

He took Zoe's hand and led her towards the car that DC Moore had parked there on his arrival. They were followed by a group of policemen heading to their own vehicles.

As the troop walked away, none of them noticed a large white bird take off from the roof of a nearby building and wing its way silently and majestically skyward in the moonlight.